MAY 15 2002

7/18

T/18

2017-1

‹ 3/17

Yellowstone Park Nurse

Also by Colleen L. Reece
in Large Print:

Alpine Meadows Nurse
Everlasting Melody
The Heritage of Nurse O'Hara
In Search of Twilight
Nurse Julie's Sacrifice

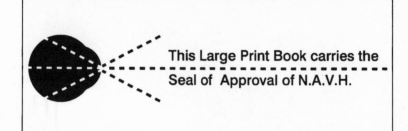

This Large Print Book carries the
Seal of Approval of N.A.V.H.

YELLOWSTONE PARK NURSE

Colleen L. Reece

G.K. Hall & Co. • Thorndike, Maine

Published in 2000 by arrangement with Colleen L. Reece

G.K. Hall Large Print Paperback Series.

The text of this Large Print edition is unabridged.
Other aspects of the book may vary from the original edition.

Set in 16 pt. Plantin by Elena Picard.

Printed in the United States on permanent paper.

Library of Congress Cataloging-in-Publication Data

Reece, Colleen L.
　　Yellowstone Park nurse / Colleen L. Reece.
　　　　p. cm.
　　ISBN 0-7838-9024-9 (lg. print : sc : alk. paper)
　　1. Yellowstone National Park — Fiction.　2. Nurses — Fiction.
　　3. Large type books.　I. Title.
PS3568.E3646 Y45 2000
813′.54—dc21
　　　　　　　　　　　　　　　　　　　　　　　　　　00-025937

Yellowstone Park Nurse

Chapter 1

Somewhere in the dark night a dog howled. Then all was still. Misty McCall shivered and pulled the covers higher. She tried to control the rising emotion filling her. It was impossible. For the first time since the funeral, the petite nurse cried. Not just tears but heartrending sobs. If those who felt Melissa McCall had held up so well during the tragedy had seen her that dark night, they would have realized how she'd been misjudged.

"Cold, emotionless," they had classified her.

It wasn't true. She had simply been too stunned by the plane accident claiming her parents and younger brother to cry. Her four years of nurse's training, ending with graduation and a degree, mocked her. What good were they? She had no one who would care — not now.

The dog howled again. This time it was not just another lonely sound, but the cry of an animal in pain. It reached Misty through her own misery more than anything else could have done. Snapping on her light, she shivered in the freezing air, snatched at a warm robe, and stuck her feet into fur-lined slippers. Her teeth were chattering from the cold by the time she slipped out of her door, down the dormitory hall, and to the outside door. She could hear scratching, then a low whine. The howls had subsided.

Taking a deep breath, Misty cautiously unlocked the door. A blast of sub-zero weather rushed in, along with a red setter. It was a struggle shutting the door, but Misty managed to extricate herself from the dog's onslaught and close it. The hall was now nearly as cold as the outdoors.

"Come on, you," she whispered.

She tiptoed back to her room. There was no use crossing over to the hospital. All the medical equipment for the coming tourist season was still packed. That's why Misty was there — to help get the hospital set up at Yellowstone Park, near the town of Lake, for the summer. She quickly discovered the dog had a sharp stone embedded in one of his paws.

The poor creature whined and limped as Misty surveyed her own first-aid kit. Good! There was a slender but strong pair of tweezers, gauze, and some antibiotic cream. These things would do quite adequately.

Gently Misty probed the paw and was re-warded by a yelp of pain when the stone came free. Then she received a rough doggy kiss from a wet tongue.

"Good boy!" She still spoke in whispers.

Hopefully Ginger was a sound enough sleeper not to hear, and Misty had heard the cook, who slept near the front door, say it would take dyna-mite to rouse her once she was asleep. The rest of the dormitory was empty. Early spring was not the time for business. It would all come later.

Misty bandaged the leg and sat back. Her first patient! What would Ginger say? The thought sobered Misty and she shivered again. Better get this dog out of here until morning before Ginger found out. Ginger might be the best friend in the world, but her temper in the middle of the night could match her red hair.

When Misty went to let the dog out, she encountered a real problem. He wouldn't go. She pushed. She pulled. She begged and coaxed. Nothing worked. She even stepped outside herself and closed the door — just after he had rushed in, leaving her on the outside, him inside!

The cold wind bit through even the warm robe she'd pulled on. In spite of that, her overdeveloped sense of humor threatened to put her into hysterics. What a first patient this one had turned out to be!

She slipped back into the dormitory, anxiously looking down the hall to Ginger's room. No sound, yet. The last thing Misty needed was a limping red setter in her room, but there seemed to be no other choice.

"Okay, you big lunk, but be quiet!" Misty said and opened the door to her room.

She didn't know if he understood, but he did follow quietly. He even lay down by her bed after licking her hand. Then he closed his eyes and slept.

The cold air and unexpected activity proved therapeutic. As soon as the warm blankets were back in place, Misty was asleep.

"For heaven's sake — what's *that?*" Jennifer Snapp's pointing finger indicated the sleeping heap of dog by Misty's bed. She had come over to wake Misty and found the unexpected roommate.

Misty came alive in a minute. The room wasn't so cold now. Evidently, Jennifer had turned up the heat. "He howled, then scratched at the door last night. I finally let him in and took a stone out of his foot. He wouldn't go back out."

"I guess not!" Jennifer roared with laughter. "He's the hospital mascot. He's used to being around here."

Misty joined the laughter at her own expense. "You should have seen me trying to force him out the door!" She thought of her struggle. "Ginger, you wouldn't have believed it!"

She saw the look of relief on the other nurse's face. For a moment Misty was transported back, more than four years, to the day she had entered nurse's training. She had been sitting rather forlornly on her bed when a tall second-year nurse had come in.

"Better not sit on the bed, Melissa. It's against the rules." Ginger threw a sharp look at Misty. "They said your nickname was Misty. I'm Jennifer Snapp, your big sister, but everyone calls me Ginger." Before Misty could more than gape openmouthed, the older girl laughed. "Yes, Ginger Snapp. It was inevitable, I suppose."

The laugh they shared was the beginning of their friendship.

Now Misty leaned back in bed, enjoying a moment of quiet. "Ginger." Her throat felt clogged. "I haven't been able to thank you for — for taking charge of me after the accident. I do appreciate it."

"Of course, you do." Ginger's eyes were the same amber color as the sleepy red setter's coat. "But it really wasn't anything. I just couldn't see you going off somewhere by yourself, trying to break into a new routine. Lucky you graduated at midterm. This season at Yellowstone Park will be exactly what you need. You'll meet all kinds of people, and when the hospital closes next fall, you'll have a better idea of what you want to do."

Ginger's brilliant smile flashed. "Besides, I just wanted to spend some time with you, and what better place than here?" She gestured toward the window.

It was beautiful outside. It might still be freezing cold, but the blue sky and bright sun gave an appearance of warmth. Never had Misty seen such a clear, unpolluted sky. No factories here to belch smoke into the air! Just tall, tall trees to tower over them, and that blue sky overhead. A little thrill went through Misty. Somehow nothing looked quite so bad today.

"We'll work unpacking and getting set up until we're tired. Then we'll get outside for a while," Ginger said.

Misty remembered her friend's promise later

in the day. Her back ached from moving supplies. Yet it was a good tiredness. One thing, she'd better gain back all that weight she had lost when the accident occurred. She needed it. Today had shown how her usual strength was lacking.

Ginger noticed and commented, "By tourist season you'll be in top shape. Nora Maloney is the best cook in the world. Just wait."

The sun was firing one parting ray when Misty stepped outside. Ginger was fastening her boots. The dog, Reddy by name, had followed Misty.

"Go on out," Ginger had called. "Be there in a sec."

Suddenly Misty wanted to run, to embrace the clean, beautiful world. And she raced down the path, Reddy at her heels. There was still packed snow everywhere, slicker than Misty realized. The next instant she was falling. Whack! Her head hit the ground with a resounding bang. For a moment she lay still, stunned.

"You stupid kid, running on ice!" The voice roared in her ear. Iron-strong arms picked her up and carried her back to the hospital, brushing past Ginger in the doorway. "Get out of my way, this boy took a bad fall. He could have a concussion!"

Boy! Whoever this was thought she was a boy! Misty gasped. Well, she supposed it was logical. The wool cap covered her hair. She hadn't bothered with lipstick. Her five-foot-two-inch frame was even slighter than usual. It was a natural enough mistake. But to be carried like that! She began to struggle.

"Lie still, won't you?" Her rescuer was pushing open the door into the room Misty had helped set up earlier. Ginger was speechless until the man turned to her. "Well, don't stand there like an idiot. Get me a towel." She obeyed, still silent.

The strange man, bundled up until he almost looked like a bear, was running water, washing his hands carefully. The reprieve gave Misty the opportunity to sit up from where she had been unceremoniously dumped on the table and to remove her cap.

"Get back down on that table!" There was no disobeying the command.

Misty meekly lay down. It was a relief after all. Her probing fingers had found a goose-egg-sized knot on her head. She was in for a bad headache if nothing more.

The doctor, for he must be one, marched back to the table. Only then did he see Misty for the first time, really see her clearly. "You're a girl!" He sounded accusing, as if she had deceived him.

"Naturally. You were expecting the Easter Bunny, maybe?"

"That's enough smart remarks out of you! Keep still and turn over." His curt reply completely took away Misty's desire to slide off the table and rush out the door. He'd probably just catch her.

"Hmmm. Skin's not broken, but you're going to have a dandy bruise." He peered into her eyes. "At least there's no sign of concussion. Good. Keep down for a few hours and use an ice bag to reduce the swelling." He looked over his shoulder at Ginger. "Know how to use an ice bag?"

Her eyes widened and a mischievous look crept into them. "A little."

"Then help her out. If she shows signs of restlessness or headache, she can have two aspirins." He stared at Ginger. "Are you intelligent enough to know if she develops any kind of symptoms that might be more serious?"

It was too much for red-headed Ginger. Her voice was colder than the frost designs forming on the window. "I ought to. I'm a registered nurse. This is my second year in Yellowstone."

He didn't look chagrined or ruffled or any of the things he should have looked. He just grunted, "Good. Call me if she shows any signs of concussion." And he stalked out.

"Well!" Misty couldn't contain herself one minute longer. Her blue eyes flashed. Then her overwhelming sense of humor came to the rescue. "Did you hear the way he said 'You're a girl!' as if it was the lowest form of creation?"

"Did I ever!" Ginger dropped to a chair. Her voice was perfect in imitating the doctor. " 'Are you intelligent enough to know if she develops any kind of symptoms that might be more serious?' "

14

The two girls collapsed with laughter, Misty holding her aching head.

Neither saw the slowly opening door. Neither noticed they were no longer alone. It wasn't until that same gruff voice put in, "I fail to find anything funny in this conversation!" that they realized the doctor had come back for some reason.

"I suggest you get to bed." His hard gaze was on Misty, but most of his anger was directed at Ginger. "If you're the nurse you think you are, you should know you don't keep a possible concussion patient on the verge of hysterics from your insulting imitations of the head doctor." He ignored their gasps. "Get her to bed and give her a light supper."

He looked at them sternly. "I can't say it's a very good start for you as a nurse."

Ginger didn't say anything.

"As for you." He turned to Misty. "Even ward maids don't make a practice of laughing at doctors — not if they want to continue being ward maids!"

Misty couldn't hold it in. Her smile was demure, her eyes mock respectful. "Thank you, sir. I really wouldn't want to lose my position — as ward maid, you know."

The doctor didn't bother to answer. He just glared again, then walked out. The slam of the door told them this time he really was gone. Or was he? Why had he come back? To check on them?

"Come on, Misty." Ginger let out a whistle. "Boy, is he ever in for a shock when he finds out you're a nurse. How were we to know he's the head doctor here this summer? You know the Livingston Clinic staffs the hospital. Different doctors come different times. This is going to be a joyous occasion if he's around all the time!"

By the time Misty was tucked in bed after a supper cooked by Nora that lived up to all its advance raves, she was a little ashamed. After all, they *had* been disrespectful. Her face burned as she relived the scene — seeing herself falling, being scooped up and taken for a boy, then classified as a ward maid. One dimple appeared in her cheek. Ginger said the girls who worked at Yellowstone as maids were the finest girls on earth. Maybe it had been a compliment instead of an insult.

Misty drifted off to sleep. But after a few hours she woke up. The ice bag had turned warm. Her head ached and she felt miserable. Yet she knew she probably did not have a concussion. She was just feeling the results of her fall. Her body ached as well as her head.

Worst of all was her overwhelming loneliness. Ginger was asleep in her own room not far away, but beyond that, everything was new and strange. How could she cope with it? Especially since she'd gotten off to such a terrible start with the head doctor? What was she doing here, anyway? Maybe it would have been better to stay in Helena where she'd trained.

But she was here now. And she must make good here, then find another job in the fall. She could feel herself getting tense and deliberately forced herself to relax. Maybe if she'd think about everything Ginger had told her of the park medical services it would help her relax.

The hospital was leased, staffed, and run by the Livingston Clinic and located at Lake, near Fishing Bridge. It would be open mid-May to mid-September. The only reason she and Ginger were there now was to get things ready. In a week or two some of the maids would arrive. Doctors came over from Livingston on a rotating basis. Good! Then this officious head doctor wouldn't be there all the time. Approximately eight nurses were used — two on duty, the others on call.

In addition to this hospital at Lake, there were self-contained dispensaries at Old Faithful, Mammoth, Canyon Village, and Fishing Bridge.

During the season, a nurse was at each dispensary at all times. Would she be sent to one of the dispensaries, or be able to stay at the hospital with Ginger?

Misty shuddered. The thought of staying alone in a dispensary was frightening. And while the one at Old Faithful was surrounded by other people, the others were not. She thought, *I hope I don't get asked to go. I'm a coward. I'm not used to the great outdoors. I wonder if I'd be brave if a real emergency came up.*

Her line of thought was depressing and she switched it. If only she and Ginger could have some free time together! In spite of her training in Helena, Misty had never been to the park before. It seemed incredible — to spend four years so close and never get into Yellowstone Park! She'd make up for it this summer when she had free time.

She reviewed what she knew of the hospital. It had a few semi-private rooms. A ward. A total of twelve to fourteen beds. Dormitory facilities for the staff, except for the doctors, who had private quarters. Sometimes the doctors brought their families and stayed a month at a time. In addition there was a permanently settled doctor at Mammoth who was on call. Some of the nurses came from as far away as Boston and other East Coast cities. It was an honor to be chosen.

For the first time a real thrill of excitement went through Misty. Here was work, challenging, meaningful work to be done. People would come in with every type of hurt imaginable. While extremely serious cases were flown to Salt Lake City, the hospital handled all the routine cases and even emergency surgery. She would be part of it all.

Misty fell asleep wondering if she were a big enough person to accept responsibility. Memory of her training and high grades reassured her. The little review had done wonders for her headache. A few moments later she slept.

Within a day or two, Misty would never have known she had been injured. The swelling had diminished considerably even after the first day. Dr. Neil Rogers insisted on looking it over. It was Misty's second mishap with the doctor. He had not mentioned his name that first day. And when he called, barking into the phone, "Young woman, get over here immediately, room 202," he hadn't told her he was Dr. Rogers, just, "This is Neil Rogers." Misty had been making her bed and finished what she was doing, then took time to smooth her hair.

Evidently Dr. Rogers was not used to being kept waiting. There was fire in his eyes when she came in. "Did I interrupt your gossiping?"

Misty's heart sank. So Neil Rogers was Dr. Rogers, head doctor of the hospital — and her boss! Fuming at the irony of it, she submitted to his examination, trying to formulate words of explanation. She might as well have saved her breath. The minute he finished examining her head, he marched out, nearly running down Ginger, who was coming into the room with an armful of clean linen.

"Well, I did it again." Misty sounded so dejected Ginger stared.

"Did what?"

"Made a fool of myself in front of our boss." She told Ginger what had happened. "Ginger, the worst thing about it all is — *if I were to meet Dr. Rogers head-on in the hall, I wouldn't recognize him!*" She caught Ginger's amazement. "Both times he's examined my head he's been so bundled up in that scarf and hat, his face has been covered. It will be just my luck to foul everything up by not knowing him!"

"Don't worry about it. Maybe he'll assign you

to one of the dispensaries." Ginger looked droopy. Since Misty had been partially incapacitated, Ginger had spent hours unpacking and putting away instruments, sterilizing them, readying all the things to be used during the tourist season.

"I've worried about that, too. Could I handle it?" Misty asked.

"Sure. Last year was my first year and I was on a dispensary part of the summer. In order to give the nurses there some time off, we try and help them out. It's kind of lonesome, but it's also peaceful when you don't have patients. Besides, we're always in telephone contact with the hospital. Anything more than immediate attention gets shipped over to the hospital in the ambulance. We don't take chances with the patients."

Her matter-of-fact tone reassured Misty. After all, if Ginger thought she could handle things, she probably could.

I'll just forget my bad start with Dr. Neil Rogers and do the best job I can. I always liked the name Neil. Too bad this one turned out to be such a grouch! I wonder what he looks like, behind that cap and scarf?

Misty laughed to herself. Now if only she could find out without betraying herself in some even stupider way than she'd already done! It was worth speculating about — especially since it was so all important that this same Dr. Rogers approve of her work. But why did she have to come up with a boss like that?

Yet even as she mentally complained, Misty remembered the careful, almost tender way Dr. Rogers's fingers had touched her head. He might be abrupt, humorless, brusque — all the adjectives she could think of — but he was also a dedicated and concerned doctor. After all, what more could she ask?

Chapter 2

Misty burst into Ginger's room. Her face was red, her eyes scared. "Ginger, what do they do to park employees who tear sinks off the walls?"

Ginger dropped the hairbrush she'd been using. "What do they do to *what?*"

Misty dropped into the chair in Ginger's room. "I just tore a sink off the wall in the doctor's lounge."

"The doctor's lounge! What on earth were you doing in there?"

Misty was struggling between laughter and tears. "Dr. Neil Rogers saw me in the hospital hall. He told me the sink in the doctor's lounge was absolutely filthy! He realized the hospital wasn't open yet, but if I was going to be here setting up, then I might as well get it cleaned up."

"And you *cleaned* it?" Ginger was incredulous. "I'd have told him to go jump in the lake!"

"I thought maybe when he finds out I'm a nurse instead of a maid, he would at least remember I followed orders." The tears threatened to spill over, in spite of the nervous giggle. "Anyway, I was really making with the cleanser when all of a sudden the whole sink fell off the wall!"

"What did you do?" Ginger was frozen to the spot.

"Left it on the floor. What could I do?"

Ginger was speechless. All the two girls could do was stare at each other. Then they exploded. They laughed until they cried, then laughed some more.

"If I only had a picture of it," Ginger choked. "Could I ever blackmail you!" She took in her pint-sized friend. "You, of all people! Tearing a sink off the wall — and in the doctor's lounge!" It set them off again.

Misty felt weak by the time they finally settled down. If she had planned to get in hot water from the time she'd arrived, she couldn't have done a better job of it!

"Wh-what do I do now?"

"No problem. Our maintenance man arrived today. I'll tell him the sink needs fixing." There was a twinkle in Ginger's eye. "Shall I tell him how it got torn off?"

"Don't you dare!" Misty caught the twinkle and decided to match it. She forced herself to look scared. "I suppose they'll take it out of my salary."

She could see Ginger hesitate. Then the red-headed nurse's desire to tease overcame her. "Probably."

A moment later Ginger was gone, leaving Misty chuckling to herself. She'd really play it for all it was worth, act scared, give Ginger time to convince her they'd take it from her salary, then have the last laugh. She wasn't too convinced Ginger would keep the story to herself, either. It

was just too good not to share — and too unbelievable.

Misty sat back remembering the pranks the
nurses had played on each other during training.
She herself had spent a frantic half hour
searching the store room for a "tourniquet for a
goiter case — a neck tourniquet" one of the in-
terns had asked for. Ginger had finally found her
almost in tears and, between gales of laughter,
told her there was no such thing as a neck tourniquet — how could there be? It would choke the
patient to death!

Misty smiled at how young and naive she had
been. Never again! Then and there she determined not to be gullible. She refused to be the
target of hospital jokes here at Yellowstone. In
fact, she'd act so innocent they'd think she was a
target, then give it back to them all.

Nora, the cook, had told Misty to watch out
for the young maintenance man. "When our ambulance driver gets here, and those two young
harum-scarums get together, watch out!"

Misty's first encounter with the two was entirely pleasant.

When Ginger came back, her eyes were sparkling. "We have a date!"

"A date?"

"Yes, you parrot, a date. Jim and Frank are
taking us to the hotel tonight for dinner *and*
dancing! There's going to be a square dance tonight."

"I've never square danced in my life!"

"You will tonight. Come on, get ready. It will be our big fling before the tourists start coming. We've been so busy lately, we haven't had time to breathe!" She slipped out of the room.

Misty reached for a dress, choosing a blue one with a full skirt. Her knowledge of square dancing was nil. She was smart enough to know she'd need a full skirt to give her freedom of movement, however.

"You look like a little girl." Ginger's approval was warm. Misty's dress just suited her. Ginger herself was clad in an old-fashioned print, russet and brown.

"And you look like an autumn leaf!"

"This will be fun," Ginger confided. "The hotel is really nice."

It was. Located about a half mile, more or less, from the hospital, it was four stories high, with white pillars, colonial style. The food was excellent but no better than Nora's. It was fun to be dressed up and on a date.

Their escorts were lean, tanned young men, both full of laughter. The maintenance man, Jim Robinson, was a typical playboy in the best sense. He would be a good friend.

Frank Jensen was a different matter. His work as ambulance driver had given him close contact with Ginger the year before. His respect and admiration shone through every look he gave her. Misty saw the answering gleam in Ginger's eye and sighed a little. If she wasn't mistaken, Ginger and Frank were either in love or very close to it. She was glad for her friend, and yet she suddenly felt left out. She'd always been too busy to really settle down with one young man.

Why the name Neil Rogers crossed her mind she didn't know. She didn't even know what the man looked like, for heaven's sake! Deliberately she turned to Jim. "I have never square danced."

"You'll be a natural. It's great exercise and fun."

It was. At first she stumbled around. But once she caught the pattern, it was easy to follow Jim. He was a superb square dancer. By the time a few figures were through, Misty was breathless but having a wonderful time.

"May I?" The dance had changed to a waltz. Before Jim could even nod, she was swept away. Misty glanced up at her unexpected partner, frowning. There was something vaguely familiar about him, yet she didn't think she'd ever seen him before. Why had he cut in on her? Who was he? He was tall, craggy rather than handsome. His nose evidently had been broken at some time, but it only added to the charm of his smile. Eyes as blue as her own were keen, piercing. When the dance was over, he led her to chairs in front of the fireplace.

"I haven't met you, have I?" She smiled at him. "I'm Melissa McCall, Misty."

"Glad to meet you. You're here for the whole season?"

She didn't notice he didn't give his name — not then. "Well, I hope so," she said.

"Oh?"

Suddenly Misty felt his compassion, his sympathy. Before she could even understand why, she was telling him everything that had happened. The plane crash. Her loneliness. Ginger's help in securing this job.

"Do you like it here?"

"I love it." Her simple words brought a smile to his face. "I can't even begin to say how much! These past few weeks of setting up the hospital, getting ready, have been hard work, but so challenging, just thinking how all these things will be needed later."

She paused. "Then, too, I've been able to get outdoors. Ginger took me to see them dynamite the ice jams under Fishing Bridge. I've never seen anything like it!" Her thin face glowed and she leaned forward. "The last few weeks of watching out the windows, seeing the frozen lake, all the snow, and then the dynamiting! Great chunks of ice exploding into the air. It must be something like the Arctic breakup. I won't forget it — ever."

"Then if you like it here so much, why are you unsure of staying?"

There was something so understanding in his voice Misty opened up completely. She didn't stop to think she had never been one to spill over her problems to anyone. She just knew here was someone who seemed to care that she had problems. "It's Dr. Rogers."

"Dr. Rogers!"

"You sound shocked. Do you know him?"

The man's face was grim. "I know him, all right. What's he done now?"

"It isn't what he has done, it's what I've done." She told him about her first meeting with the heavily bundled doctor, how he'd mistaken her for a boy. She told of his further mistaking her for a maid, how he'd barked at her to clean the sink in the doctor's lounge.

"I cleaned it, all right. It tore completely off the wall!" He roared, but she wasn't through. "He doesn't even know I'm a nurse. When he finds out, I don't know what I'll do! He will probably judge me on past performance. I'll never get a chance to prove I *am* a good nurse. The bad thing is — I don't even know what he looks like! The two times I saw him he was all bundled up. I have no idea what I'll find when I do see him!"

Was her woman's intuition trying to tell her something, or was she just suddenly aware of talking too much? She could sense a struggle within the man beside her. "If you want to go ahead and laugh, it's okay. I probably talked too much, but I'm really concerned about it. It's terribly important for me to make good here. Not just for my record, but for myself. I've gained some weight, and now I'm ready to take on whatever is coming. I only hope things will be all right with Dr. Rogers. We heard that for the first time there will be one doctor at the hospital all summer, with others rotating in. Dr. Rogers will be my boss. I have to make good."

The tall man stood, noticing Ginger and the two men were coming their way. "I'll put in a good word for you with Dr. Rogers, Miss McCall. Thank you for a pleasant" — he paused — "and enlightening conversation." He smiled. The next moment he was gone.

"Why'd your friend run away?" Ginger wanted to know. "How'd he happen to be talking with you, anyway?"

"He cut in on a waltz. Then we came here." Misty shrugged. "The fire felt good, and we just got to talking. He's one of the park rangers, maybe?" She was thinking of the feeling of trust the man had inspired in her, and the confidence. Was he married? She grinned at her own question.

"Some park ranger!" Jim snorted, bringing Misty back to reality. "You honestly don't know who that is?"

"Of course not! How could we?" Ginger was indignant. "We don't hang out the windows trying to find out who every Tom, Dick, and Harry around here is."

Frank slapped his knee. "Is that ever rich! Wait until Dr. Neil Rogers gets wind that you girls consider him a Tom, Dick, or Harry!"

"Neil Rogers!" Ginger's exclamation echoed Misty's whisper. She noticed her friend's white face. "Misty, are you all right?"

Never had Misty been called on to pull herself together on such short notice as she now had. Dr. Neil Rogers. Her boss. The words beat dully in her mind. "I guess it's just a little too much excitement. Maybe I'd better call it an evening."

Ginger looked at her suspiciously, but agreed. Something certainly was wrong with Misty. What had she said to Dr. Rogers? She hadn't known who it was, that was obvious. It wasn't until they were back in Misty's room she could ask. Whatever it was didn't concern Jim and Frank.

Misty looked much as she had four years earlier, huddled forlornly on her bed, facing something new and strange. Ginger felt sorry for her, dreading something unknown, even as she had felt sorry for the younger Misty on her first day of training.

"All right, let's have it," Ginger said.

"You'll never believe how stupid I've been!" Great sobs broke through Misty. "He seemed so kind, so understanding. He wanted to know if I liked it here, if I was going to stay. I told him it depended on Dr. Rogers!"

"You didn't!"

"Yes, I did. He laughed about the sink, and about my being taken for a boy, and about everything. Probably laughed all the way back to his home and my dismissal papers!"

"What did he say when he left?"

"He said he'd put in a good word for me with Dr. Rogers, and thanked me for a pleasant and 'enlightened' conversation!"

Ginger didn't answer for a moment. When she did, it was quietly. "Misty, I don't think you have anything to worry about. Did he seem sarcastic, or angry, or anything?"

Misty shook her head. "No. In fact, when I told him my staying depended on Dr. Rogers, he wanted to know what he had done now."

"And you told him."

"I told him."

"Well, if after all that, he didn't seem angry, I wouldn't worry about it." Ginger was trying to be cheerful. She didn't add what she intended to do. Misty had been through enough without this added to her problems. "I'll get you a glass of warm milk and you get some sleep."

Misty didn't see the tablet Ginger dissolved in the milk. She was surprised she could fall asleep so easily.

When she awoke it was late and she knew it. Before she could get up, Ginger burst into the room.

"You look like the proverbial cat," Misty said. "Is that a canary feather sticking out of your mouth? So you slipped a sedative in my milk."

Ginger didn't even seem to notice. "Get up and dressed. Dr. Rogers wants to see you immediately."

Misty's heart sank. "How do you know?"

She didn't notice how evasive Ginger's answer was. "Oh, I ran into him in the hospital."

If she had known of the earlier interview, her

hands would not have shaken as she dressed, hastily pulling on warm clothing. She had not been prepared for such an early summons.

Neither had Dr. Rogers been prepared for an even earlier meeting with her friend. He had barely shaved and dressed when the knock came. Who on earth? He opened the door to a bundled-up figure.

"May I come in?" Before he could answer, Ginger was inside. Throwing back her parka hood, she faced him squarely.

"Oh, it's Miss . . . Snapp, is it?"

"That's right. Jennifer Snapp. Yellowstone Park Hospital nurse and friend of Melissa McCall."

"I already knew that."

"I'm glad you did. It will save time." Ginger's chin was tilted to a belligerent degree.

"Did she send you?" Was that disappointment in his tone?

Ginger didn't wait to decide. "She did not. She's sound asleep from a sedative I slipped in her milk last night. She needed the rest."

Dr. Rogers felt a warm approval for this worthy adversary. "You realize nurses are not in the habit of pounding on doctors' doors demanding admittance, don't you?"

"Maybe they should be."

The doctor's eyes narrowed. He was hugely enjoying this but wouldn't have let on for words. "I could have you fired for insolence, Miss Snapp."

"That's why I'm here. When you make out dismissal papers on Misty, you can make mine out along with them."

"You'd give up your job for your friend?"

Ginger's eyes were cold, hard. "I'd give anything to keep her from being hurt anymore. What's a job compared to a friend?"

Dr. Rogers couldn't keep his admiration back any longer. He held out a strong hand. "Good for you, Miss Snapp! By the way, I have no intention whatsoever of recommending Miss McCall for dismissal."

"You haven't?" The hand within Dr. Rogers's clasp went slack.

"Of course not. As I told her last night, our conversation was — quite enlightening. Now if you'll ask her to come over when she's dressed, please."

There was dismissal in his voice, but Ginger didn't care. Her warmth was as easily roused as her anger. "You're a doll, Dr. Rogers!"

Before he could recover, she was out the door, running down the path across the gravel road and through the trees to the long, low dormitory building.

It wasn't quite a half hour later when Dr. Rogers received his second caller. This knock was timid, not demanding.

"Good morning, Miss McCall. Won't you come in?" He ushered her into the room.

She had time to notice it was attractively furnished and very neat before he motioned to a

33

chair. When she sat down it was on the chair's edge.

"I thought we might take a few minutes to go over the duties you will be performing this summer. For the first part of the summer, at least, I prefer to keep you and Miss Snapp both here at the hospital. Later, one or the other of you will probably be helping out in one of the dispensaries."

Misty didn't hear much of what he was saying. Words trembled on her lips, but she had to swallow hard to get them out. "Then I'll still be here?"

Dr. Rogers put on a surprised look. "Well, I certainly hope so! You told me you liked it here and wanted to stay. You haven't changed your mind, have you?"

She could barely force out the word. "No."

"Good! We need you desperately." He went on explaining how the setup worked and ended with, "I suppose you and Miss Snapp would like to have the same shift, at least at first? This will give you time off together to see the park."

There was no denying the glow appearing in Misty's eyes. "That would be wonderful."

"Then it's settled." He stood, dismissing her as quickly and painlessly as he had dismissed Ginger a short time before.

Before she knew what she was doing, Misty found herself outside his door, remembering his smile as he'd said, "I'll be seeing you, Miss Mc-Call."

In a daze she walked down the path, across the gravel road, and through the trees. She did not run as Ginger had done. She just walked, slowly and without seeing.

"What happened?" Ginger was dying to know whether Dr. Rogers had given away her earlier visit.

"He told me he thought he'd keep us together here, at least at first. He's giving us the same shift so we can have time off together."

"He is! How nice." Ginger could hardly believe her ears. "What else did he say?"

"Just that he hoped I hadn't changed my mind about staying." She stared at Ginger. "*Me* change my mind? Not a chance." She shook her head. "He isn't at all what I had expected."

"Me, either." Ginger caught herself hoping Misty hadn't noticed the little slip. She hadn't. "I guess we'd better go see if Nora will give us some breakfast."

"Good idea."

As the two nurses stepped from the dormitory to walk the few feet separating them from the hospital building, Ginger smiled to herself. *I didn't think he'd give me away — and he didn't.*

Chapter 3

The tourists had arrived. Almost overnight the silent, empty hospital was filled with people. Misty had been right. Nowhere else could she have gained the experience she would on this summer's job. If there was any cut, bruise, burn, or fall a tourist could manage, someone was sure to come in with one!

Late one afternoon she dropped down in a chair at the nurses' station. She was tired, really tired. It seemed they had been flooded with patients during the afternoon. She glanced at the clock on the wall. Good! Just a few minutes more and she could head for the shower, get into sports clothes, and go outside.

From the reception room in front of the hospital, as well as through some of the semi-private-room windows, Yellowstone Lake had been sparkling enticingly all afternoon. Now all she wanted was to get outside, cross the highway, and get down where she could lean back against a tree and enjoy watching the lake.

The phone rang. It was Frank. "Misty? I'm bringing in a patient. Have a gurney at the ambulance entrance. Tell Dr. Rogers this one will require surgery; it's a man with a badly gored leg."

He hung up before Misty could ask, "How could he get a gored leg?"

Misty knew Dr. Rogers had just left for his own home. She dialed. "Dr. Rogers? Nurse Mc-Call. The ambulance is bringing in a badly hurt patient. Frank Jensen says he'll require surgery."

"I'll be right over."

He was. Misty had barely hung up the phone when Dr. Rogers strode in. He saw the faint blue shadows under her eyes. She looked tired.

"I know you're scheduled to go off duty, but could I get you to help? We're going to need a team and some of the other nurses are away."

She never hesitated. "I'd be glad to help. But what did Frank mean by gored?"

"Probably by a buffalo."

"A buffalo!" Misty could scarcely believe her ears. "Do buffaloes attack people?"

Dr. Rogers's jaw was grim. "Not if people remember they are wild animals." He caught Misty's look of surprise. "I can tell you exactly what happened. In spite of our signs to stay in cars, keep away from wild animals, this man probably left his car, took a camera, and marched out toward the buffalo herd. Buffalo will usually just move away, but if one feels threatened, he may charge. Once he does, there's no outrunning him."

"But why don't the tourists obey the signs?"

Her question must have struck a nerve with the doctor. He scowled. "For the same reason you no longer see many bears in Yellowstone. We've had to pack them all off into the wilds — simply because people *would not leave them alone!* I've seen supposedly intelligent people place a tiny child in front of a bear, move back, and take a picture. I've seen them trying to pose bears, telling them to 'Get back, so I can take a picture.' I've seen them feed and harass bears until someone gets hurt. That's why much of Yellowstone's charm has been lost. If people had kept garbage covered and their hands off the bears, things wouldn't have been ruined!"

Before Misty could answer, the wail of the ambulance alerted them. Frank swung into the drive. Almost before the motor stopped, he and Dr. Rogers were gently lifting the patient to a gurney.

Frank's face was white. "He got it pretty bad, Dr. Rogers. He tried to take a picture." Misty lost nothing of the exchange of glances between Frank and the doctor.

"Trying to take a picture," the doctor echoed.

So Dr. Rogers had been right. Misty saw the look of restrained fury at the man's stupidity replaced by professional concern mingled with compassion. The victim's face was ashen.

"Fortunately he passed out just after I got him in the ambulance," Frank said. He nodded to the pressure bandage. "I stopped the bleeding and got him here immediately."

Dr. Rogers was already on his way to scrub. "Help Misty get him prepared, will you, Frank?"

Misty looked up in surprise, but Frank didn't notice. He was already expertly slitting the rest of the pants leg, gently undressing the man.

It seemed an incredibly short time before Misty, gowned and sterile, was passing instruments to Dr. Rogers. Frank had been right. It was a nasty wound. Dr. Rogers's fingers clamped, tied, sutured. Even so, it took a long time.

Misty was exhausted when they were finished. Ginger would special the patient through the night. The main worry now was how much blood he'd lost. He had evidently been alone when the accident happened. A passing motorist had found him and had had presence of mind enough to get to the nearest emergency phone and call an ambulance.

"I hope his picture was worth it." Misty looked at the doctor, noting the regret in his voice. "That patient will limp for the rest of his life because of today's little picture excursion." He finished cleaning up and walked out.

But when Misty noticed Frank was still there, she understood far more than the doctor had said.

Frank's face was serious. "The poor guy's lucky at that, you know. If Neil Rogers weren't one of the best surgeons around, that patient wouldn't make it at all."

Misty hurried through her cleanup and slipped to the dorm. Since the maids had come, and also other nurses, Ginger had moved in with her. It worked out fine since they were usually both on the same shift. Now Ginger was already with the patient, and the room was empty. Misty smiled at the neat way Ginger's side of the room looked. She wasn't normally so tidy herself.

But Ginger had told Misty, "If I live with you, I'll keep things picked up. I know you hate clutter."

A few minutes later found Misty under a tree, watching the double attraction of the setting sun reflected in the lake. She'd been too tired to eat. She had wanted to get outside, breathe some fresh air, be away from sickness for a while. After a bit, even the lovely sunset faded from her sight. For she had fallen asleep. She awoke, a little chilly. Evidently her tired body had claimed rest. She sat up, stretched.

"So Sleeping Beauty decided to open her eyes."

She was wide awake instantly. The tall man who looked down at her was laughing. Dr. Rogers! Was this going to be another faux pas?

He seemed to catch her feeling. "Sit still, Miss McCall. Best thing in the world for you. And what better place?" He gestured over the lake. The sun had gone. In its place was the promise of twilight. There was almost a purple glow in the shadows, and a tipsily quartered moon peered down.

"I really love it here." The spontaneous little outburst rather embarrassed her. Was she always to act like a child when with the doctor, except when on duty? She knew he recognized her nursing skills. If only she could feel as comfortable when off duty!

"I'm glad." The breeze springing up ruffled his hair. "It's one of the most beautiful places on earth."

"I know. Even though I haven't seen a whole lot, why, this is enough!" She broke off and laughed. "Funny, when people talk about Yellowstone, they always talk about Old Faithful or sometimes the bears that used to be here. They don't even mention the lake, or trees, or all the other beautiful scenery!"

"Have you seen the Paint Pots? Or Roaring Mountain? Or Yellowstone Point?" he asked.

"Not yet."

Dr. Rogers seemed to consider for a long moment. "Perhaps you and Miss Snapp would like to make the Loop some Saturday."

She hesitated, not quite knowing how to break through the shock she felt. Dr. Rogers asking *her* to go anywhere?

He mistook her silence for refusal and sighed. "Then again, perhaps you wouldn't." He walked away, then threw back over his shoulder, "By the way, be sure and go in the staff dining room and get some supper. I told Nora you'd be late."

In another moment he'd be gone. Misty recovered her wits and stood. "Dr. Rogers . . ."

He paused, impatience in the way he turned toward her.

"I'd love to make the Loop some Saturday."

For a moment she was stunned by his changing expression. Even in the dim light she could see his annoyance change to a smile.

41

"Good. We'll arrange it." This time he didn't walk off but waited for her. "In the meantime, I think I'll catch another cup of coffee while you eat."

Silently they walked across the highway, still now except for occasional cars, and up through the parking lot. Misty experienced the familiar thrill that always went through her when she approached the one-story hospital. It was so complete, so compact, hugging the ground. From the reception area a small hall went left, past the linen rooms and doctor's lounge to the operating room. Straight ahead was the nurses' station, with a forked hall leading left and right. Left was the ambulance entrance and emergency room. There were also the kitchen, staff dining room, and storage rooms. On the right were four semi-private rooms, plus a ward at the end with four beds. It was all glassed in. The ward wasn't used much. But it was kept ready in case there was an emergency.

Misty gave a little sigh of happiness. "I never walk over here without wanting to pinch myself and see if it's really true. No matter what other jobs I have, I know this first one at Yellowstone will never be replaced in my memories."

Dr. Rogers looked at her intently through the growing darkness. Sincerity rang in her every word. "Miss McCall, I've been wondering whether you might consider making this area your permanent working place."

"How could I?" The tourist season ended in

42

mid-September. She'd been there long enough to know that. "The hospital isn't open during the winter."

"I know." She had the sneaking suspicion he was laughing at her, but he kept it from his voice if he was. "There's a new angle. The doctor who is a permanent resident at Mammoth is thinking of an early retirement. He's been there for years. He has quite a practice built up. You know, Upper Mammoth is open all year round. There's an inn, and a lot of the park employees are there. Lower Mammoth has housing for the government employees, and a school. There's even a church at Mammoth."

"But where do I come in?"

"I'm seriously considering taking over the older doctor's practice. If I do, I'd like a qualified nurse."

"You mean me?"

Again she had the feeling he was laughing at her. "Well, I consider you and Miss Snapp the best nurses here. She already has a job in Gardiner. You know, that's only five miles from Mammoth. You could see each other often."

They had reached the dining room. Conversation was at a standstill as Nora fixed a plate for Misty.

When they were served, Dr. Rogers continued. "There's only one thing. I should warn you we get all kinds of snow. We'll be called to go out in snowmobiles. There are those who wander off, get lost. Another thing would be your living quarters."

"Living quarters?"

There was a twinkle in the keen blue eyes. "There's a girls' dorm there, but it's mostly for the maids and those who work at the inn. That leaves two choices. One would be a small log cabin. It would be a little primitive, but livable."

A log cabin! Live in a log cabin? Somewhere in Misty's past there had been a pioneer. It was this ancestor's spirit now glowing in her eyes. "A log cabin sounds different." She couldn't know how attractive she was to the man across the table. "What's the other choice?"

"There's a nice doctor's residence at Mammoth that goes with the practice. You could always share that, of course." He ignored her gasp and calmly added sugar to his coffee. "You'd have to marry me. I couldn't afford to have my reputation tarnished. Besides, I wouldn't want to."

Flashes of rage and amusement went through Misty. Of all the unexpected, conceited . . . She ran out of adjectives. Before she could even open her mouth to tell this brash doctor exactly what she thought of him, Ginger came in.

"Dr. Rogers, could you come look at our patient?" The redhead looked apologetic. "He seems restless. I'd like to increase that painkiller dosage if it's all right."

Instantly the earlier conversation stopped. Without even looking at Misty, Dr. Rogers followed Ginger out. Smallness was one of the pluses of the way the hospital was built. It didn't take long to get from one area to another.

Well! Misty dropped her fork, gazing unseeing at the tasty dinner Nora had given her. Even the aroma of her favorite roast beef didn't rouse her. So Dr. Rogers could offer marriage as casually as if he'd asked her to pass the salt! His reputation! She was furious. What about her own ideals? He hadn't even asked about them! But her sense of humor was too great. Taken at face value it was the funniest thing she'd ever had happen to her. Her very first proposal! She had always dreamed how it would be — a romantic, shadowy setting, perhaps a garden. A hero who would become serious, plead with his eyes. Even though she recognized her daydream for what it was — an idle fantasy — Dr. Rogers's proposal was just too much by contrast.

Misty started to giggle. Luckily only Nora Maloney was around and she was rattling pots and pans in the kitchen. Misty was free to laugh until her sides ached. Wait until she told Ginger!

On second thought, she wouldn't tell Ginger. Not just now. She'd wait until some time in the future when she could think it all over a little more. Besides, there were other things to think of. She'd been offered a job by a doctor whose skill she admired tremendously. She'd been offered the chance to live in a log cabin. Most of all, she'd been offered a way to be close to Ginger, just five miles apart. Why, they could have a ball!

Ginger had already told her of the winter fun

around Gardiner. She could be part of it! What more could she ask? When Dr. Rogers asked again if she'd like the job, she wouldn't need to hesitate. She'd tell him yes.

There was a demure look in her eyes. She could just picture it, telling him she'd take the job — but had decided to take the log cabin over his other choice. Her eyes flashed with laughter. She could hardly wait for him to approach her again.

He didn't. The next few days were so busy with various patient ailments and first-aid treatments there was little time for any of them to think of personal matters. When there finally was a little break, it wasn't long enough to go into any type of humorous spiel.

Dr. Rogers approached her at the nurses' station. "Have you had an opportunity to think about the job, Miss McCall?"

There were others around. All she could say was, "I'd like it very much."

"Good. I've made final arrangements to take over the practice. I'll let them know I have my own nurse." He smiled.

"I'm not doing anyone out of a job, am I? As nurse, I mean?"

"No. The doctor's wife is an R.N. She has helped him all these years." He turned away, then back. "By the way, Miss McCall, I'll be driving up Saturday to look it over again. Would you care to ride along?"

She managed to hide the thrill inside. "Yes, I

would. I can look at the log cabin." For a moment she caught the flash of fun in his eyes and thought he was going to say something, but he only nodded and walked away.

"So you're going to Mammoth with Dr. Neil Rogers Saturday." Ginger yawned. She'd had a hard day. "Good. You'll have fun."

"You mean we. He said originally he would take us both."

Ginger shook her head. "Not me, not this Saturday. I'm going on a hike with Frank."

"You mean I'll be spending the day alone with Dr. Rogers?"

"Well, for heaven's sake! You sound like someone's maiden aunt. Haven't you ever spent a day alone with a man before?"

Misty could feel her face redden. "Of course, but not with someone like Dr. Rogers."

Ginger grinned impishly. "I'll bet you a dollar it's Neil and Misty before you're twenty miles from here!"

Misty remembered Ginger's taunt and bet on Saturday morning. It was clear, bright. It was also a bit chilly at first. She was glad for the windbreaker she'd tossed over her turquoise pants suit.

"Dr. Rogers, it's nice of you to take me with you."

"Why not make it Neil away from the hospital?"

Misty smiled. "No reason. Oh, by the way, how far have we come?"

He looked at her in surprise. "Let's see — twenty-one miles. Why?"

"I just wondered." Her mind was busy. So I won the bet, by one mile! She forced back the bubble of laughter threatening to burst.

"I thought we'd go by way of West Thumb and Old Faithful. We can come back past Norris junction and Canyon Village. Another time I'll take you up past Tower Falls and through Dunraven Pass. It's really beautiful."

Misty caught his words "another time" and smiled. Something warm filled her. Was there any reason she shouldn't let go and like this doctor, now the ice had been thoroughly broken? As far as she knew, he was a fine person. She firmly shoved the idea away and settled back to enjoy the day.

There were miles of trees and winding roads. The inn at Old Faithful, with its two hundred rooms, loomed above her, and she enjoyed meeting the nurse on duty in the dispensary there. Most of all she enjoyed the erupting of Old Faithful. All the pictures in the world hadn't prepared her for the feeling of awe as the rumbling began, increased, and culminated in the world-famous explosion of hot water and steam into the sky.

Neil Rogers didn't watch the performance. He watched Misty. He took several snapshots of her with the camera he'd brought along. It had been years since he'd been interested in a girl. One bad experience had soured him. But she was different, as different as her name. She was so natural, so sweet. He caught himself. Better get off that line. She was also the kind who would have a hundred guys after her! He scowled, disliking the idea.

"I can't even begin to say anything." Misty turned from the spectacle, but not until after every bit had diminished, leaving only wetness to show where it had been.

She was thrilled the same way over and over as they went on. Mammoth was a busy place.

"It's just as busy in winter," Neil told her. "I was up here last December. It really hums."

"I think I'll enjoy working here." She was wide-eyed.

The retiring doctor and his wife had insisted on them staying for lunch. And, upon Neil's request, the doctor took a snapshot of Neil and Misty. Now he chuckled. "You'll set this place on its ear, young lady!"

"Melvin!" his wife reproved him. "Don't tease the doctor's girl."

"But I'm not . . ." Misty caught the twinkle in Neil's eye. "I'm not sure how I'll fit in with all the ice and snow. We had a lot of it in Helena when I was in training, but I originally came from southern California."

Her little ruse worked perfectly. Neil asked, "How'd you ever decide to train in Helena?"

"My aunt was a nurse. She trained there and left money in her will for my schooling. She said it didn't have strings attached, but if I would consider it, she'd like for me to train in Helena. I checked the credentials. It was an excellent school. It seemed little enough to do for her, even though she never knew."

Neil Rogers shot a glance at her. The next question from the friendly doctor or his wife would probably be about Misty's parents. He stood. "I hate to rush off, but we have a lot to do." He knew by her little sigh of relief Misty had feared further questions, no matter how kindly or well meant.

"We'll be seeing you again before winter, I hope," the retiring doctor said.

"Of course. For one thing we have to get Misty moved over here after the hospital closes."

Misty was silent as they walked to the car. Then she said, "They're really nice, aren't they? Did you notice, all these years together, and they're still in love?"

"I noticed." There was a grim line to Neil's jaw. Misty couldn't know that for one moment when they had gone through the pleasant home he had wished with all his heart she would be living in that home with him. He snorted to himself. He was no teenager to develop a crush. He had his work, his path cut out for him.

Yet even Dr. Neil Rogers couldn't have explained satisfactorily that feeling he had experienced sitting across the table from Misty in the home so full of love. One thing he would bet his life on — if or when Melissa McCall, R.N., fell in love, it would be for keeps. None of this on-

50

again, off-again stuff for her. This time there was no denying the pang that shot through him at the thought: *What if it is with someone else?*

Chapter 4

"Miss McCall! Miss Snapp!" Dr. Rogers's voice preceded him into the dining room. The two nurses had been grabbing a quick cup of coffee. The hospital seemed a beehive. It was Sunday afternoon, and all kinds of patients were coming in. Many of them had only needed first aid, but one man was resting easily after a mild heart attack.

"I'm going to be needing you both." Dr. Rogers dropped wearily into a chair. "They're bringing in a badly burned college boy — he's been hot potting!"

Ginger's face turned white. "Oh, no! Not that again." Seeing Misty's look of surprise, she explained. "We get a lot of college-age kids up here. Some of them work for the park, others are simply tourists. A favorite sport is hot potting — slipping out after it's dark and going swimming in one of the pools. Many of them are lukewarm, great for swimming. The others . . ." Her voice broke off at the sheer horror in Misty's face.

"You mean . . ." Misty swallowed hard. "Sometimes they get in the wrong pools?"

Ginger's face was grim. "That's exactly what I mean. If they have been drinking, they stumble into the boiling ones." She forced a steadiness to her voice. "Some of the time they test it with a

52

hand or foot first. They are burned badly but know what it's like. One last year didn't test it. He dove into the pool. He was flown to a burn clinic in Salt Lake City, but we heard afterward he didn't make it. He was burned too badly."

Dr. Rogers's fist hit the table. "It ought to be stopped!"

Ginger nodded. "That's right. But how? Every hot geyser or spring is clearly marked with many signs warning people to stay on walks, to keep away. People are stupid. They don't pay any attention to the signs. The park has done everything in its power to prevent this kind of accident, and still there are those who persist in killing themselves by their own stupid actions!"

Ginger's eyes blazed. "You can't patrol every inch of this park every minute of the day and night. The Park Service, the park employees — everyone does all they can. But if you are bound and determined to go your own way, you're going to wind up hurt, or dead. That's why the bears are back away from the tourists. People just wouldn't leave them alone. We had accident after accident." She looked at Misty. "Even in the time you've been here, we've had how many accidents involving animals?"

"A lot." Misty was sober. "Not one of them would have happened if people had obeyed the park rules."

"That's right. It all boils down to a bunch of ir-responsible people who won't believe anything can ever happen to them. It will always be someone else who is hurt." She stopped for breath, but before Misty could say anything, the ambulance drove into the driveway. Instantly the three were on their feet. By the time Frank had the door open, they were there.

"This one's lucky." Frank's face was as sober as Dr. Rogers's had been when he told them about the hot-potting victim coming in. "He slipped out at daybreak. Evidently he'd been drinking, but he did know enough to test it first. When his foot hit that water, he got it out as soon as he could. He had a long way to crawl to get help. Why he chose a hot pot miles off the road, I'll never know! Anyway, it took him all morning to get where he was going and back to the dispensary at Old Faithful. He didn't even make that. I guess the pain finally got through until he couldn't go any farther. He must have lain within just a few hundred feet of Old Faithful for several hours. Finally he was discovered in a grove of trees and they got him to the Old Faithful dispensary and called me." Frank clenched his teeth. "I hate burn cases. They're so ghastly."

Misty echoed Frank's sentiments when she gazed at the exposed foot. Dr. Rogers had cut off the shoe, leaving a mass of raw flesh. In spite of all her training, she thought for a moment she would be sick. Thank God the young man was still unconscious! Every inch he had crawled with that foot must have been agony. Was Frank right? Had he been drunk? The fact he still had on his shoe, had tested the water with it on, seemed to corroborate it. The shoe had protected part of his foot, but the canvas had also held in the heat. His foot was a mess.

"He will live, but he may lose that foot." Dr. Rogers's forehead was beaded with sweat. "We can do an emergency amputation if we have to, but I hope it won't be necessary."

For three days and nights the young man's fate hung in the balance. Misty, Ginger, and the other nurses took turns specialing him. Dr. Rogers spent as much time with him as he could. Mercifully, the young man seemed much better on the fourth day.

"I think he's going to be all right." Dr. Rogers's face was lined. "We're getting a helicopter in to fly him to Billings. He'll fly to Salt Lake City from there. We've done all we can. But this young man will carry scars on that foot for the rest of his life."

The doctor's shoulders slumped. "I guess people will never learn."

Misty's eyes were suddenly moist as the usually brusque doctor went out; his shoulders drooped. So he wasn't as tough as one would think. Why it should send a thrill through Misty she didn't know, or wouldn't admit. But in the time since she'd been working in the hospital she had learned to admire Dr. Rogers tremendously.

"You like Dr. Rogers, don't you, Misty?" Ginger had just come in from spending a little off-duty time with Frank and was in a rosy glow. If all worked out, they would be married the following summer. She was inclined to see the world as a romantic place. Now if Misty would just get interested in someone!

"He's a fine doctor." There was reticence in Misty's reply.

Even Ginger couldn't go beyond it. Somehow a little wall had suddenly sprung up between them on this one subject. It answered Ginger's question better than words would have done. Misty *did* like the doctor, a great deal. Ginger smiled to herself. There was nothing like summer, working together, and the beauty of Yellowstone Park to promote falling in love! She hugged her own happiness close.

Next year Frank would be through with college. He had started late, working a few years after high school. Perhaps it was this sense of responsibility that had drawn Ginger to him the summer before. He was going to school during the year and working summers driving an ambulance. He had wanted to be a park ranger naturalist since his first visit to Yellowstone Park, when he was ten years old. Now the end of the dream was in sight.

Ginger smiled again. Frank would be a fine ranger naturalist, but the hospital would lose a good ambulance driver. When he knew he would be driving an ambulance, he voluntarily took all the first-aid courses he could find, even studying on his own to be of service to those he carried.

It had been said by park personnel that Frank Jensen was the next best thing to a doctor. Yet inside he hated the pain and suffering he carried, those who accidentally or willfully were hurt. It would be good when it was over.

Misty saw the dreamy look in her friend's eyes. Again, that same pang went through her. Was it loneliness, envy? How would it feel to be in love, really in love, and planning to marry someone? Dr. Neil Rogers's face swam in her mind and Misty could feel hot color creeping up from her white collar. Luckily Ginger was too far gone in her own thoughts to notice.

A few days later Misty had call to wonder even more. She glanced out the window and noticed one of the maids slipping toward the doctors' homes. There was no reason the maid shouldn't be there. She had probably been sent for. It was more the way she walked that caught Misty's attention. Furtively, casting glances behind her, as if she didn't want to be seen. She disappeared into the trees, leaving Misty wondering. But there wasn't time for curiosity. There was work to be done.

Misty had all but forgotten the incident until Ginger asked her a few days later, "Misty, have you noticed anything strange about that new maid? I think her name is Marge something or other."

Misty looked up from the uniform she'd been repairing. A button had been loose. "I did see her acting rather strange about going over to the doctors' quarters. I figured she'd been called to do something."

Ginger shook her head. "The maids clean over there now and then, but as a general rule they aren't called. I wonder what she was doing? The reason I ask is I caught her mooning around making a nuisance of herself when Dr. Rogers went off duty today. He looked mad enough to chew nails." She frowned. "You know, the maids are great, but this new one is something else. I don't know if she'll last. She's absolutely man hungry."

"Ginger!"

"She is. She's been throwing herself at everything in pants since she got here." Ginger warmed to her subject. "I even caught her in one of the patient's rooms making a fuss over a good-looking male patient. You know the maids don't have patient contact. When I told her she shouldn't be there, she just smiled and said she was sorry. She had noticed we didn't have aides so she thought we might be able to use someone to help cheer up the patients. Cheer them up! Raise their blood pressure more likely! That skintight clothing she wears is just too much!"

Misty was shocked. It wasn't like Ginger to be bitter about anyone. Marge really must have been insolent to bring on all this. "Maybe she's just lonely."

"Well, she'd better get it in her head the hospital isn't a social club and keep her entertainment for off-duty."

Misty thought of what Ginger had said a few days later. Again she saw Marge slipping through the trees toward the doctors' quarters. The girl's face flashed in the sunlight just before she stepped behind a tree. Was she meeting someone?

Misty never could have told afterward what impulse led her to quietly step outside and follow, being careful not to make any noise. She wasn't the nosy type, but there was something in that girl's actions spelling trouble. If she really were a troublemaker, the hospital could be upset. Maybe not. Anyway, Misty would see what she could find out.

Stepping slowly and quietly, Misty kept the girl in sight. Sure enough, she headed straight for the doctors' quarters. Misty held her breath and followed, getting within earshot. Straight to Dr. Neil Rogers's home Marge went. Once she was out of sight of the hospital, her furtiveness left her. Only boldness was in her swagger as she tucked her snug sweater into her snug jeans and rapped on the door.

Dr. Rogers opened it. Misty could hear his voice perfectly through the clear air. "What are you doing here, now? Did anyone see you come? You were supposed to wait until night."

Misty was frozen by the words. Mad enough to bite nails, Ginger had said. Dr. Rogers certainly must think he was the world's greatest actor to pull off something like this. He knew Marge. He had expected her to come, even though she had evidently disobeyed orders. Misty lost Marge's answer in the fog of pain and disillusionment that swept through her.

But Dr. Rogers's reply was loud and clear. "When I got you the job you agreed to —" The closing door shut off the rest of his sentence.

Somehow Misty stumbled back through the trees, hoping she wouldn't run into anyone. Luck was with her. The area outside the hospital was deserted. Ginger would be in their room now. She couldn't go there. Without thinking, she crossed the road and walked to the big tree overlooking Yellowstone Lake. For a moment a pang went through her.

The last time she had been there, Neil Rogers had found her, had offered to take her sight-seeing. She closed her eyes. Memory after memory flooded through her. Dr. Rogers saying, "I'll put in a good word for you." Dr. Rogers saying, ". . . make this area your permanent working place." Dr. Rogers saying, "You'd have to marry me. I couldn't afford to have my reputation tarnished."

Wave after wave of shame went through Misty. So he had been lying when he added, "Besides, I wouldn't want to." He had probably been laughing at her, supremely confident of his male superiority. Perhaps he had seen she was beginning to admire him. As a doctor, she hastily added to herself. But was it only as a doctor?

Misty remembered something else. On the way to Mammoth she had wondered if there was any reason she shouldn't let go and really like him. She had her answer. No matter how modern the world was, Misty still had ideals. Now even to herself she couldn't admit how terribly crushed she was to find out Dr. Rogers was just like all the others.

So he had got the job for Marge, brought her up here with some kind of understanding between them. An understanding that Marge would act as if she didn't know him in front of others, evidently. But the thing that hurt most was not how angry Dr. Rogers had been at Marge for coming to his home, *but only because she had come at the wrong time!*

A bitter smile crossed Misty's face. He must never know she had begun to put him on a pedestal. Lancelot and King Arthur and all her childhood heroes rolled into one. Would she betray herself in front of him? What if she came upon Marge hanging around as Ginger had described from that other time?

There was no way to avoid it. Misty wouldn't give up her job in this place she had come to love because her idol turned out to have clay feet. She would just have to keep her feelings to herself.

Ginger wondered a few days later what had happened to Misty. "Are you getting too tired? I know you've volunteered for extra duty."

"No, I'm fine." But the shadow in Misty's eyes was a giveaway to Ginger.

The redhead didn't force the issue, but she

knew something was troubling Misty. She even discussed it with Frank.

"Maybe she's working too hard," was Frank's reaction. "The first time we're free, let's take her somewhere special. Maybe Dr. Rogers would like to go with us. He seems like a good guy. I also noticed he keeps a pretty sharp eye out for Misty."

Misty was strangely indifferent to the plan. "I think I'd rather just wait awhile. We're so busy and everything." Her voice trailed off.

Ginger took the hint. Something had happened between Misty and Dr. Rogers. Where she had been eager to see and do everything, now she was listless. Only on duty did Misty seem fully alive. Some of the hard-earned pounds she had gained from Nora's cooking were lost.

There were times when Misty could feel Neil Rogers's eyes on her face, but she never dreamed he would go so far as he did. Catching her on her break one evening, he laid down the law.

"You've been working too hard, Miss McCall. Get outside and spend more time in the fresh air. We have enough patients in this hospital without our staff being sick. You'll be the next patient if you keep on as you are."

Misty hated herself for the warm glow filling her at his concern. She stilled her trembling fingers and looked straight at him. Her voice was cool. "Please don't trouble yourself about me, Dr. Rogers. I am perfectly able to judge what condition my health is in."

She walked away, leaving him flabbergasted, perhaps for the first time in his life.

What had changed her? She had always been eager, and after they had straightened out those early difficulties, she had even been friendly. He had hoped she was learning to like him. Now there had been only a remote, disinterested look in her face.

Dr. Rogers wasn't one to let things go. He hunted Ginger up. "What's wrong with your friend these days?" he asked.

Ginger didn't pretend. "I don't know. I thought maybe you did."

"Me!" he exploded. "What makes you think I have anything to do with Miss McCall's moods?"

"I just thought maybe you knew." Ginger had already learned what she wanted to know by his question. He evidently was concerned about Misty, far more than a doctor would be about a good nurse. He was also obviously puzzled.

He was even more puzzled a few days later when Misty sought him out. There was still the same faint dislike in her eyes as she said, "I think I'd like to get some experience at one of the infirmaries. You said we'd need to trade off and help out the infirmary nurses. Is there an opening?"

His cool tones matched her own. "There is. The nurse at Fishing Bridge needs some time off. I can arrange for you to take over for her if you like."

"That would be fine."

Something of his puzzlement and hurt shone through his reply. "I thought you liked it here."

"I do. I just think it would be nice to try something else now."

There was nothing more for him to say. "We'll get you transferred this Saturday, if that's what you want. It's only a few miles from here to Fishing Bridge. If you need me at any time, you'll only have to call."

"That will be comforting, I'm sure." There was no sarcasm in her voice. There was no emotion whatsoever.

It infuriated Dr. Rogers. "What's wrong with you, Miss McCall? You have about as much spark as a robot these days!"

All the shame, disappointment, and pain Misty had suffered burst forth. "I'd rather be a robot than a — a pasha!"

Before he could answer, she was on her feet. He was quicker than she was, reaching the door and barring her way. "Just what is that supposed to mean?"

Misty had never seen him so angry. A white line rimmed his lips. His hands gripped her arms until she knew there would be black and blue marks from his fingerprints. She wouldn't dignify the situation by struggling. Neither would she answer. Let him figure it out, he was so smart.

The door swung open, framing a girl in tight clothing. "Did you call, Neil? I mean, Dr. Rogers?" Marge's smile was a smirk, her knowing eyes taking in the little picture before her.

"No, I didn't call! Get out of here!" His roar could have been heard in the adjacent dormitory. Marge just smiled and closed the door behind her.

Dr. Rogers looked back at Misty, who had used the interruption to free herself from his grasp. He caught the accusation in her shadowed blue eyes, the scorn on her face. He also caught a glimpse of something else in her eyes. Was it sadness?

Before he could recover, she said simply, "I'll leave Saturday. Good-bye, Dr. Rogers." And she was gone.

He was left staring at the door, his thoughts whirling. He took one giant stride as if to follow her, then stopped. Whatever it was, perhaps it would work out better to let her go — for now.

In his unsuspicious male way, he never even vaguely guessed why Misty had requested the transfer. He was not conceited where women were concerned. He had no way of knowing Misty was leaving because she could not trust her secret if she stayed. He only knew when the door closed behind her, something precious had stepped from his life.

In a typical masculine manner he vented his rage at the nearest object. "Marge, get in here!" There were a few things he wanted to say.

Chapter 5

It's a whole different world. I don't know if I will like it. Misty's thoughts were as bleak as the view from her tiny window. Ginger had assured her the rain was unseasonable. It would probably stop in a day or two. It hadn't. In the week Misty had been at the Fishing Bridge dispensary, it had poured. At times her spirits were as gray as the outside world.

It's so isolated. Not even to herself could Misty admit how upsetting it was to be all alone in the little dispensary, away from others. At the hospital, at least she had others nearby. Here when she awoke in the night, hearing strange noises, there was no one across the room.

Never had Misty been in such a situation. She had always been surrounded by people. Here she was one hundred percent on her own. Some pioneer she was! She almost lay in wait for patients, keeping them as long as they would visit. There was a place for a patient to lie down and rest for a few hours if necessary. So far only one woman had used it. She had overexerted herself on the trail and was brought in exhausted.

"I wonder if I really want to work at Mammoth this winter?" Misty's voice sounded loud in the empty room. She had arranged and rearranged the drug cabinet, carefully checking against the master list to see that everything was in order. The few possessions she used daily were neatly placed. "At least it would be busy. But I'd be working every day with Neil." She didn't realize she had used his first name.

Memory flashed through her — Marge in her tight outfit. She couldn't be over a scant eighteen. Dr. Rogers must be in his late twenties, at least, perhaps even in his early thirties. What could he see in the girl who was holding herself so cheaply?

"Surprise!"

Misty hadn't heard the car drive up. "Ginger!" She had to blink to hide the tears. She'd never been so glad to see anyone in her whole life. "How did you get here?"

Ginger's knowing eyes caught the unusual eagerness. She wisely kept still. There had been some reason for Misty wanting to come out here and be isolated, but it would have to come from her. "Oh, I had a day off and I asked Dr. Rogers if I could borrow his car and come see you."

"You did!" Misty couldn't keep back the delighted grin. "He loaned it to you?"

"He sure did. He also said to tell you the hospital misses you, and whenever you're ready to come back, he will assign another nurse here."

Misty couldn't have kept her heart from bouncing up to her throat if her life had depended on it. Her casual answer was a mastery over self. "How nice of him." She deliberately changed the subject. "How's everything at the hospital?"

"We're in the middle of a slack season. Rain and tourists don't mix well. That's how I could get off."

The day was long and satisfying. Because of the weather, and because Misty was on duty, they stayed inside and just talked. Of the past and their training days. Of the present and their jobs. Of Ginger's future. Nothing was said about Misty's future. If Ginger noticed her friend's reticence, she didn't comment. After all, how could they discuss it? The last Ginger knew, Misty was all set for Mammoth. Since Misty herself didn't know what her final decision would be, there was no point in bringing it up.

It wasn't until late afternoon that Misty voiced the question she had been wanting to ask all day. "Is that maid, what's her name — Marge — getting along any better?"

The only description of Ginger's inelegant answer was a snort. "Are you kidding? She's the only inadequate maid Yellowstone has ever hired, as far as I know." Ginger looked puzzled. "I don't know why she is kept on. You'd think someone would get rid of her. I thought for a while Dr. Rogers was going to throw her out, but he didn't. The whole hospital's talking about her and the way she acts."

Ginger hesitated, not knowing if she should go on. Yet Misty should know the rest, especially if she were thinking of coming back to the hospital.

"They're also wondering why Dr. Rogers puts up with her. He just isn't known for long suffering and all that! I really thought Marge had had it the day you left. I saw her come out of Dr. Rogers's office crying. Not ordinary tears, but real mad ones. He must really have bawled her out for something."

Misty's unpredictable heart rose, then dropped. "And still he didn't fire her?"

"No, and I sure can't understand it. I overheard him say, 'You've been nothing but trouble since you came here. I wish I'd never consented.' I don't know if he knew her before, or what, but it's sure funny." Ginger couldn't stand the misery in her friend's face. She hastily changed the subject. "By the way, we have a mystery at the hospital. Someone's stealing stuff. Money, small pieces of equipment, anything."

Her words were an effective wet sponge across the blackboard of Misty's mind. "What!"

"Yes. We have a thief."

"Do they have any idea who's doing it?"

Ginger looked a little strange. "I have an idea, but it's based on prejudice, so I won't tell you now. Dr. Rogers is absolutely furious. The last thing we need is someone like that. They even stole some of the medications." She paused, wondering how to warn Misty.

She thought of what Dr. Rogers had told her just before she left for this visit. "Tell Misty to be on the lookout, but don't scare her. Anyone smart enough to know there's a dispensary is also smart enough to know it will contain some good equipment, and a thief can be unpredictable."

"It really isn't anything to be too concerned with, Misty, but be a little careful. You know it's just possible some idiot might think of stealing the equipment and drugs here."

Misty's face turned white. Just what she needed — something else to think about when she heard noises in the night.

"Well." Ginger stood. "I have to get back. I wish you'd transfer back, Misty. Our room is lonely without you." She laughed. "I'll bet not as lonely as here. I remember last year. The first few days, I was petrified to stay alone. Then I got used to the peace and quiet." She waved and ran through the rain, a gallant figure in her emerald green raincoat, red hair uncovered. When she went, she took with her the last remaining bit of brightness from the gloomy day.

"What am I going to do?" Misty whispered. "I'm scared and lonesome. What if someone should break in here, a thief?" She shook herself and forced her unwilling hands to prepare a simple meal. It was hard to swallow the food.

The night was one of horror. The rain stopped and the moon came out. With it came night rustlings of all sorts. Was it animals coming out after the rain? Or was it something more menacing, some human?

When Misty finally awakened, it was with a feeling she had not slept at all. How much more of this she could stand she didn't know.

The afternoon brought another visitor. It had started to rain again, and Misty didn't know when she ushered in a dripping Dr. Rogers why he had come. She had no way of knowing about the conversation between him and Ginger the day before.

"How's your friend?" Dr. Rogers had asked Ginger across a small table in the dining room.

"I think she's lonely, scared, and determined to overcome it."

"Why doesn't she just come back to the hospital? Not every nurse is equipped to work alone in a dispensary, especially when it's isolated from other people the way ours are. There's no disgrace in fearing the unknown. She's a city girl. This is all new to her."

Boy, Ginger thought, he's really given this some consideration!

He wasn't through. "I'm from the country myself. The first time I got sent down to a crowded slum in a big city during training, I was so scared I wanted to run. I remember my heart beating so loudly I knew everyone on the street could hear it. I forced myself to do my job, but I hated it. When I finished my training and internship, I decided to spend the rest of my life in some out-of-the-way place where there weren't any city streets."

Somehow his confession endeared him to Ginger. He hadn't been ashamed to admit he'd been scared. Impulsively she leaned forward.

"Something is bothering Misty. I have no clue what the real problem is." He didn't catch the way she stressed real. "Maybe she's trying to prove something. She was plenty scared when I warned her to keep an eye out and said that we had a thief. She didn't let it faze her, but I'm wondering if she slept at all last night. Why don't you run over and check on her?"

"If I can get away, I will."

A few hours later, Dr. Rogers was walking into the Fishing Bridge dispensary. His professional eye caught the dark shadows under Misty's eyes, resulting from her sleeplessness.

"I think I'd better order you back to the hospital, young lady. You don't look too well."

A flare of color touched Misty's face. "Thanks a lot, Dr. Rogers. I don't need to be ordered anywhere. I can take care of myself."

"Oh, can you?" He saw her anger and dropped his voice. "I didn't come over here to fight with you, Miss McCall."

"Then why did you come?" The question hung in the air between them. Dr. Rogers stared at her. Why had he come? Simply because Ginger had requested it? He was too honest to pass it off so simply.

Misty's face flushed. Why had she ever asked such a question? After all, he was her boss. If he chose to visit the dispensary without warning, that was his privilege.

Neil noticed the drooping lips. Suddenly he wanted to kiss those lips more than he'd wanted anything in a long time. He took one step toward her, then caught himself. What a fool he was! She didn't even like him. If he kissed her now , it would wreck any chance even of renewing the friendship that had been forming earlier in the summer.

Stung by his silence, Misty brashly repeated her question. "Just why did you come?"

"I came to find out what you meant by your rather unusual statement the day you asked to be transferred!" It was out in the open now, hanging between them.

Misty made no pretense of misunderstanding. "You mean why I called you a pasha."

The angry light in his eyes should have warned her. "That's right."

She shrugged. "You know the answer better than I do. You were the one to bring Marge to Yellowstone." She clapped her hand to her mouth, wishing she'd never said it. It was so ugly, even if it was true.

Neil Rogers's face had turned to granite. "So that's what you think of me! Why —" He seemed unable to continue. Then he said, "Nothing could be further from the truth!" He stared at her as if she were repulsive. "You actually thought I asked that child to come here because I cared for her?"

Misty forced her heart back in place. Wild hope had gone through her at the disbelief in his voice. There had been truth in his voice, blazing truth. *What had she done?*

In a dim haze she could see him advancing toward her. She backed away from the terrible anger in his face, anger at what had evidently been an unjust accusation.

Now his voice was soft. "So that's what you think of me. Well, now you'll have something more to think about."

She was in his arms, held tightly. The kisses he rained on her face were hurting, punishment for her lack of faith. At first she struggled. It was no use. Her small frame lacking in strength was no match for him.

Gradually his anger subsided. The last kiss was tender, almost gentle. It tore the veil of shelter from Misty's heart as nothing else could have done. Another moment and her arms would have been around his neck. Her lips would have betrayed the love that had evidently been in her heart all along. But in that moment he thrust her from him. His voice was mocking, his eyes bitter. "Now when you think of me as a pasha, at least you will have some justification. You'll have to admit, though, it was fun while it lasted!"

The door slammed behind him. Misty stood huddled against the wall. She felt as if she were being pulled apart. The womanhood of her gloried in the love that had filled her, the love to which she had looked forward from childhood. It also taunted her. How despicable she had been! She should never have judged by appearances. He hated her for her lack of trust. What could she do?

Hours later, she dropped off to sleep. Her bed was rumpled from her tossing and turning. Yet that one last, gentle kiss was her last waking memory, the rest of it mercifully tuned out by her body's demand for rest.

Dr. Rogers had driven off in the rain, cursing himself. Why had he acted as he had? Why should he care what Melissa McCall thought of him? His jaw was set, his eyes hard. Let her think what she would. It didn't make any difference.

His fist smashed down on the dashboard. "But it does!" The gesture, the putting it into words, brought it all out. The days she had been gone, the coolness between them, the memory of her former friendship followed by dislike when he looked at her, had broken his iron self-control. To think, she actually thought — he couldn't go on. He had been cut deeply by her lack of trust. Marge! The spoiled little trouble-maker! Why had he ever agreed to get her a job up here?

He thought of his sister's white face. "If you don't find a place for her, I don't know what will happen. She's running with a wild bunch. She used to adore her Uncle Neil when she was small. You might be the making of her, Neil."

Surprisingly enough, Marge had fallen right in with the plans. She had been thrilled at the chance to work at Yellowstone Park. She knew it was an honor. Young people from all over the country were hired. If she wanted to go because of what she'd heard about boys and thrills, she kept it to herself.

"I should pack her off back home, right now." But Neil Rogers's hands were tied. He had agreed to give Marge a chance. Her parents were using the time for a long-deserved vacation. He couldn't send her back until the end of the summer. She had no other place to go.

He hardened his heart against the look of Misty as he had seen her last, looking at him in a way he couldn't begin to interpret. He'd tried to help a kid, and this was his reward! People, meaning Misty, thought he was in love with the brat!

"Did you see Misty? Is she coming back to the hospital?" Ginger asked, running toward him as he entered the hospital.

"I saw her. No, she won't be coming back for a while." He marched past her, leaving Ginger staring wide-eyed.

Boy, he looked like death and destruction, the redhead thought. What on earth had Misty done to him? Ginger hated to do it, but she had a report to make. "Dr. Rogers."

"Yes?" It was one note below an absolute growl.

"We did another drug count. Some pills are missing."

Instantly he was all doctor. Personal problems were secondary to this. "How many?"

"An entire box."

He closed his eyes and sighed. "Anything else missing?"

"I don't know. I also don't know how we can stop the stealing. You know, the other times only a few pills were taken. And some instruments and money. Now this."

Neil Rogers looked at her more closely. "Miss Snapp, do you have any idea who is doing this?"

His direct question caught her off guard. If she'd only had a warning, she would have been able to hedge. Now all she could do was say, "I have suspicions, but they are unfounded."

"Miss Snapp, I want to know what those suspicions are." He saw her hesitate, weighing her words. "You know as well as I what this could mean. We have to stop this. As soon as possible."

His gaze held hers.

Slowly Ginger drew something from her uniform pocket. It was the wrapping from some of their medications. "I found this in one of the maid's wastebaskets."

Neil Rogers stared at it as if it were a poisonous reptile. "How? Whose?" His face was even more deathlike than when he had come in from the rain.

"I had been suspicious of this particular person for other reasons. Today when I found what was missing, I went into her room."

"Whose room was it, Miss Snapp?"

"The newest maid's. The one called Marge." Ginger had never seen such a spasm of agony cross anyone's face as she saw now. She involuntarily reached out to him. "It may not mean what we think!"

He was white to the lips. "I'm afraid it does." For the first time Dr. Neil Rogers looked beaten. "Is that all, or is there something else?"

Who was this girl to make the doctor look like this? What was between them? Ginger forced her thoughts back to his question. "She has been meeting someone. Several times I heard her slip out of the dorm at night. Once she almost ran into me as I was coming in from night duty. This afternoon after I found this, I watched her. She slipped out through the woods past the doctors' quarters. I followed. I hated myself for playing spy, but I knew what you just said. We have to stop this stealing.

"She met a tall, bearded fellow in a yellow poncho. It was evidently not the first time, from the way they greeted each other." Ginger didn't add how Marge had flown into the stranger's arms, kissing him, clinging to him. She didn't need to. Neil was aware of his niece's ways and shocked by them at times.

"She gave him a package. I had seen enough. I thought I'd be sick, even though a nurse is supposed to be aloof from all that. I came back, and you came in."

"Will you ask Marge to come here?"

It took Ginger time to locate the maid. She finally discovered her in the ward. "You are wanted in Dr. Rogers's office immediately." In spite of her anger for what the girl had done, Ginger felt sorry for her. White-faced, defiant Marge followed the nurse to the office.

"Miss Snapp, I want you to stay, please," Neil said, then turned to the girl. "There is a serious charge against you. Miss Snapp found this in your room." He held up the wrapping from the medications. "A supply of pills were missing again today. And other things have been stolen, too. Miss Snapp followed you to your meeting place. What is he, this friend of yours?"

Marge's cold eyes stared at them both. "I don't know what you're talking about. She's just mad. She hates me because she's a friend of that doll-faced McCall babe that was here."

"That's enough!" Dr. Rogers was on his feet. Before Marge could stop him, he snatched the shoulder bag from her arm.

"Give that back, that's mine! You have no right to take that!" She was fighting, scratching, clawing like a wild animal. He held her off with one hand. With the other he unclasped the bag and dumped it on the floor.

There, lying amidst a broken compact, stubby lipstick, and loose change was the damning evidence — some small pieces of surgical equipment — very recently stolen, no doubt.

Ginger stared in horror. Even though she had suspected it, the reality of the scene was worse than anything she could have imagined. She turned toward Marge who was frantically scooping up all the things, trying to force them back in her purse, babbling incoherently. Evidently she had taken some liquor to bolster herself to do the stealing.

It took both Ginger and Dr. Rogers to get her subdued and into a room. When she had finally fallen asleep, Neil turned to Ginger. "I don't know what I would have done without you. I was wrong in bringing her here. I suspected she'd taken alcohol, but she kept it to herself. This is going to kill my sister and brother-in-law. I'll have to recall them from their trip. Maybe they can get her somewhere for professional help, before it's too late. She'll have to stand trial for the theft, too."

Ginger was stunned. "Your sister and brother-in-law? Then Marge is your niece!"

"Yes." For a moment he nearly broke. "I remember how she was a baby and toddler. Now this!"

Ginger could feel his agony. Everything began to fall into place. No wonder he had been concerned. No wonder he'd been trying to help Marge. His niece. It was still almost unbelievable.

"The important thing is to find the bearded man in the yellow slicker." Ginger's words brought Dr. Rogers back to the present. She was right.

His fingers dialed a number. Within minutes he had made his report. "The fellow has a good supply of things to sell. He'll be looking for more when they are gone. It's important, no, mandatory he be captured before that happens."

Neil cradled the phone and turned to Ginger. "They'll be on the alert. He shouldn't be suspicious, though. After all, he didn't do the actual stealing. It will be this very lack of suspicion that will trap him. He won't know anyone saw him. They think they can move right in and get him. He's probably connected with the hotel, either employee or guest."

They didn't catch the man. When they checked and found from the description he was probably Lee Crandall, who had been employed by the hotel, they went to his room. Everything was gone except a yellow slicker.

Chapter 6

The hospital was filled with tension. Three days had passed since the escape of Lee Crandall. No word had come of his capture. Dr. Rogers had teetered on the edge of recalling Misty to the hospital from the dispensary, then had rejected the idea. In some ways, she might be safer where she was. He had alerted her to possible danger, insisting she admit no one who looked suspicious.

At the end of the third day, the call came. A young man fitting the general description of Lee Crandall had been stopped at the west entrance of the park.

"Thank God!" Dr. Rogers's relief was heartfelt. Now they could get back to the business of taking care of their patients, instead of keeping half their attention on another possible problem. He surprised Ginger by stopping her in the hall. "You have a few hours off today, don't you?"

"Why, yes I do." She looked surprised. "But if you need me for anything, I'll be glad to stay."

"It's not that." He looked a little schoolboyish, then drew himself up straight. "I thought you might like to use my car and go see Miss McCall. I'm sure she'll be relieved to get a first-hand report on everything that's happened." He carefully kept all emotion from his voice, but Ginger understood.

"I'd like that very much."

A few hours later, Ginger drove to the Fishing Bridge dispensary. Misty met her at the door. She had lived through torture the past few days. Not so much from fear of the possible attempt of a thief to break in, but from mixed emotions caused by Neil Rogers's visit. Fortunately she had few patients during the afternoon. One small boy came in with a fishhook in his hand. Ginger helped Misty remove it and dress the tiny wound. A man had slipped and turned his ankle, but there was no sign of a broken bone. With instructions to soak it and keep it elevated, he hobbled off, regretting the accident that would shorten his vacation.

"Now. Tell me everything." Misty hadn't been able to get it all filled in from the brief phone conversations they'd had.

"First of all, Marge is Dr. Rogers's niece, as I told you on the phone." She couldn't know how Misty had reacted to that bit of news. Wave after wave of shame had gone through her, mingled with gladness. Dr. Rogers had been truthful. He wasn't interested in a kid in tight pants, except to try and help her.

Ginger stretched, tired from the strain of the past few days. "It sure surprised everyone. Some of the hospital staff had even wondered just what she was to Dr. Rogers." The red in Misty's cheeks gave her away. Ginger held back the words, "Were you one of them?" It was obvious Misty had wondered, along with them all.

"Evidently the girl's been heading down a wild path for a long time. The parents were about at their wits' end and asked Dr. Rogers to bring her up here and keep her out of trouble. Instead, it backfired. She's in more trouble than she bargained for."

Ginger leaned forward, eyes blazing. "Misty, she's one of the worst patients we've ever had. She's been drinking alcohol — and possibly taking some pills. She also had a touch of the flu. And is she ever sullen! You can't even get near her without her blaming everyone except herself. She just clams up when we mention Lee Crandall. I caught sight of her eyes today when Dr. Rogers told her they think Crandall's been picked up at West Yellowstone. She looked as if she'd been hit. But all she said was, 'Crandall? Oh, yeah, he's the one I was supposed to have given those things to, huh?' as if she didn't know anything!"

"It must be pretty awful to have gone through all that when you're barely eighteen years old! What kind of parents does she have?"

"I don't know, yet. They are due in the end of the week. It took time to get them back from their trip. What an ending! We are holding her in one of the semi-private rooms. Dr. Rogers doesn't trust her at all. He told me in private it would be just like Marge to try and slip out if she could. She knows her parents are coming. The staff's watching her all the time."

"Why did she do it? Why steal?"

It took Ginger a long time to answer. "I really am not sure. Maybe because she's lonely and desperately needs someone. I would guess from the way she threw herself at Lee she thought she was in love with him. Maybe it seemed a big deal, coming up to the park, falling in love with someone she met, stealing things from the hospital. I don't know. What makes anyone choose such a rotten way of life?"

Misty was sober. "I guess we were the lucky ones, Ginger. Our parents were strict but loving. They gave us something to live by, a reason to exist, a desire to find real happiness. I don't want to preach, but I think my faith in a God who cared kept me straight."

"Me, too," Ginger said. "From what Dr. Rogers told me, Marge's folks are nice but permissive. They believed you shouldn't deny your children anything. Too bad in following that trend they denied Marge the one thing she needed — a sense of responsibility."

Long after Ginger had gone, Misty thought of their chat. She had had time since coming to the Fishing Bridge dispensary to really sort out some of her own beliefs, her ideals for living. Why, I have as many planks in my foundation for living as some campaigning politician! I didn't know until I got out here away from everything just how strongly I felt about a lot of things!

It was almost a revelation to her. Her heart sank. Too bad that revelation hadn't come sooner, before she made that terrible accusation to Dr. Rogers. Her lips still burned from the memory of his kisses. How could she ever face him again? What would his reaction be? One thing for sure, she had killed any chance of ever staying at the park during the winter ahead. He wouldn't want to work daily with a nurse who had been so suspicious and who had condemned him on the basis of a few overheard words.

Where should she go? Was there demand in Gardiner for another nurse? She bit her lip, uncertain. The summer was slowly moving forward. She would have to make up her mind soon. If only something would happen to help her know!

The following Saturday night Misty had a call. Dr. Rogers's voice was professional, totally without emotion. "Miss McCall, I felt I should let you know. Lee Crandall has escaped. I don't know how, but he evidently made a break several hours ago. I wasn't notified until just now." He caught her gasp. "Don't be alarmed. There is little or no chance he will come back in this direction. It would be stupid when he has the choice of every other way to go and stay free. Yet there is the off chance he might try and contact Marge. I wouldn't put it past her to do any fool thing if he does!

"If you like, I'll send someone over for you. You can come back to the hospital until he's caught. We'll just close the dispensary."

"We can't do that." Misty was positive on that point. "There are people here who need care when accidents happen." She swallowed the fear in her throat. "I'll stay, Dr. Rogers. I'll be all right. I always lock everything at night, anyway. Probably by morning the authorities will have recaptured him."

"I hope so." There was a long pause. "If you're sure this is how you want it —"

"I'm sure. If I were an army nurse I wouldn't desert in the face of an enemy, would I?"

Dr. Rogers's voice had a strange note in it. "No, Miss McCall, I am sure you would not." Before she could respond, he had hung up, leaving her staring at the phone, hearing the rising wind outside and wondering if she had made the right decision.

She would not desert. That didn't mean she wouldn't be scared to death until the man was caught again! And she worried about Marge. She had known about juvenile delinquents, had worked with some while she was in training.

On sudden impulse she reached for pen and paper. If Marge could only know as she herself did, it might make a difference. She began to write, ignoring the growing storm, the crashing of small tree branches, even the beginning of torrents of rain. This was perhaps the most important letter she'd ever write in her entire life. It would require all her attention.

The same mail that brought Misty's letter to Marge Crawford also brought another letter, a single sheet of crude paper stuffed in a plain envelope, addressed in a scrawl. If Dr. Rogers or Ginger had seen that envelope they would never have given it to Marge. It was wrinkled, unstamped, and smelled of the earth that smudged it. But the girl who sorted the mail was in a hurry that day and didn't notice. She just tossed the two letters in the open door to the scowling Marge and called out, "Mail call!" before going back to her other work.

Marge snatched at the envelopes. She didn't recognize the writing on either, but intuition told her who had written the second letter. She heard Dr. Rogers outside her door and stuffed the envelopes in her blouse. He didn't come in. He was on his way to see a patient who had a ruptured appendix.

Marge had heard all the commotion the day before. She wrinkled up her nose. Doctors and nurses. Who needed them? That's the last thing she'd ever be.

When she was alone Marge pulled the envelopes back out, ripping open the wrinkled one. It said:

I KNOW THEY'VE GOT YOU, BABY. IF YOU CAN GET OUT, MEET ME BY OUR TREE ASAP. BRING WHAT YOU CAN.

There was no signature. There was no need for one. Marge's heart raced. So he was here!

She'd rejoiced when she overheard Ginger and Dr. Rogers talking about his escape. Deep inside

88

she wondered if he would come back for her. She'd done everything he asked her to, proved her love even by snitching stuff, but she hadn't been sure of him. A great leap of emotion inside sent red to her face. He loved her then, really loved her. She'd get out of here, meet him, and together they'd split. No one would ever find them. He had money, she'd seen to that. The only reason he'd taken the Yellowstone job was to get away from the cops who were after him, just cooling it for a while.

Marge was so excited about the note, she almost forgot the other letter. Finally she tore it open, glanced at the signature. *Misty.* That doll-faced nurse who was ga-ga over Uncle Neil? Why would she be writing? Curiosity almost overcame her hatred, but not quite. She had better things to do than spend her time reading some preachy letter. Neil had probably put Misty up to writing, trying to get on the good side of her.

She tossed the letter to the bedside table and went to stand by the window, schemes running through her mind. How could she get out of this place long enough to meet Lee? She no longer had the flu. But she was like a prisoner here. If only she had been more cooperative, they might have let her out for a walk. Was it too late?

Marge suddenly heard Dr. Rogers step out of the room next door. "He's going to be fine, Miss Snapp. The antibiotics are doing their trick. It was a close one, though. If we hadn't removed that appendix when we did and cleaned up all that infection, he wouldn't be here now."

A little shiver went through Marge. The man in the room next door had almost died!

"Uncle Neil."

Dr. Rogers stopped in surprise, peering into Marge's doorway, kept open so she could be observed at all times. She certainly sounded different from the way she had since she came to the hospital.

"Would you come in, please? And could Miss Snapp come, too?"

What now? Ginger's eyebrows sent a message to the doctor. More tricks?

Marge caught the glance. It steeled her determination to trick them. "I wanted to apologize for the way I've acted. I know you've had to keep me in here. I'm really sorry for what I've done."

She pointed to the letter on the table, the unread letter showing Misty McCall's signature. "I got a letter from Miss McCall today. She told me how much you love me, Uncle Neil. It made me feel awful." Great tears glistened in her eyes, then spilled over and down her face.

"I never should have got mixed up with Lee." Her lips trembled, her eyes swept down, hiding the gleam of triumph at the look of understanding she had glimpsed on her uncle's face. "He told me he was desperate for money for — for his mother. He was so convincing. I liked him, and I thought maybe I could help him by — by stealing some things."

She realized she had struck a false note when

Ginger raised her head and looked straight at her.

"Anyway, I just want to say I'm sorry!" Marge flung herself in Neil's arms, crying as if her heart would break.

Neil was amazed. Could Marge really be sorry? For a moment she reminded him of the way she'd been while little, running to him for comfort after being punished mildly for her own selfish actions. "It was a pretty serious thing, Margie."

Her heart leaped. When he called her Margie it meant he was weakening. "I know. I'm sorry." She stopped, then bravely lifted the chin covered with running tears. "I don't know what they'll do to me, but I'll take my medicine. When it's all over, I'm going to straighten up. Maybe go into nurses' training so I can help other people." It was an inspiration of the moment.

Marge had seen how impressed Dr. Rogers and Ginger had been when they caught sight of Misty's signature on the letter. Now she played it for all it was worth. "The nurses have been so good to me even when I've acted hateful. Maybe someday I can make up for it."

Neil melted. Ginger was a bit more reserved, more inclined to wait and see. But at least when they left her room Marge knew she had made an impression. She continued to do so, all day long.

At last she asked wistfully, "It's awfully hard just staying in my room. Isn't there something I could do? How about office work for you, Uncle Neil?"

She seemed genuinely anxious to help. Neil thought for a minute. "Why, yes, I could use some lists of patient names copied. Do you type?"

"No, but I have really good handwriting." She scrawled something on a page. She was right. Her writing was neat and clear. Besides, she would never know he didn't need the lists at all.

"You may come to my office right after dinner. Our receptionist has been too busy to do these particular lists."

Could anything have been more perfect? Marge dropped her eyes, afraid her expression would give her away. It was almost too simple. He didn't seem suspicious at all.

As soon as she finished dinner, Marge appeared in his doorway. "Your new secretary's here!" There was such an obvious change in her, Dr. Rogers almost gasped aloud. Instead he gave her the long lists, asking her to make two copies.

The industriously bent head brought a pang to him. What a girl she might have been if only she had been given useful work sooner! Maybe it wasn't too late. He would do everything in his power to help her.

He busied himself with some work of his own, wishing he could be home. Yet it was important to be here with her. If he went home he'd have to send her back to her room where she could be watched. The clock hands crept on. Six-thirty. Seven. Seven-fifteen.

Her fingers cramping from the unaccustomed writing, Marge wondered if things would work out the way she'd planned after all. If only some emergency would happen! Could she conjure up something to get rid of Neil? She didn't have to.

Five minutes later Ginger stepped to the doorway. "The appendectomy patient isn't responding well, Doctor. Could you come, please?"

He was on his feet, halfway to the door, when he remembered Marge. "You'll stay here and finish the lists, Margie? I have your promise?"

Her glance was reproachful, almost humble. "Uncle Neil! Do you think I'd try anything else — now?" He was in too much of a hurry to see that it was a question instead of a promise.

"All right. I'll be back when I can."

The minute he was out the door, Marge dropped her pen. She forced herself to wait ten whole minutes, every second ticking in her brain. Her mouth felt dry. Her hands were sweaty. She heard people hurrying back and forth. The emergency she'd wished for must have come about. An odd feeling filled her. *I hope the man lives. He provided cover for me to get out of here.* It was the first concern in all her eighteen years of life for another human being — and it was based on gratefulness for her own selfish benefits!

When all was still outside the office door, she tiptoed there, checked the hall both ways, and slipped off. In a matter of minutes she was out the front door and running.

She slowed down on the gravel. No use making extra noise. The shelter of trees swallowed her. She was free to run, exultingly, eagerly to the tree that had become her own. He would be there, waiting. His kisses would be on her lips. She felt an explosion inside. She was free, free, free!

He was there. But there were no kisses. Only a roughly snarled, "Did you bring anything? Money, or anything I can sell later?" Panting in her exertion, Marge leaned against the broad tree trunk.

Lee grabbed her shoulders. "Well? Have you got something for me?"

"I couldn't take anything more." The fingers sank further into her flesh. "Stop, Lee! You're hurting me! I was lucky to get out, let alone try for anything. But I have another plan."

The reddened eyes in the bearded face stared hard. "What is it?"

She twisted free and threw herself against him. "We'll get away from here. I'll help you get money, help you steal, if you need it. There's an emergency at the hospital. By the time they miss me, we can be gone."

"You mean go away, you and me?"

"Yeah. From now on, we're together."

She didn't notice how Lee pulled back from her, or how his lips curled. If she had, she might not even have understood. She was too caught up in what she wanted. "I couldn't take anything here. They're watching everything like crazy."

They couldn't head for town. People would be on the lookout. They would have to get far away from here — as fast as possible — by some unexpected route.

Marge thought a moment. Then she said, "I know where Neil keeps the keys to his car."

Three minutes later they were headed toward Fishing Bridge.

Chapter 7

The color of the man on the table slowly returned. It had been a close call. Even the antibiotics in his system hadn't been quite fast enough to keep the terrible infection from the ruptured appendix from polluting his body. His heart had been weak for a long time. This new complication had nearly been too much.

"He will pull through." Dr. Rogers's forehead glistened with sweat, evidence of the fight he and the others had fought for the man's life. For a few moments they had thought he was gone. It had taken an injection powerful enough to kill or cure to make their patient respond.

"Do you want me to do special duty tonight?" Ginger asked.

Neil Rogers looked at her, seeing faint shadows under her eyes. The strain of the past days showed. She had been so faithful in watching Marge, and . . . Marge! He had forgotten her. An unwelcome premonition of trouble touched him as he strode down the hall to his office. He glanced at the clock. Nine-thirty. He hadn't realized how long it had taken to bring the sick man around.

Funny, Neil could swear he had left his office door open. It was closed now. When he swung it open and flipped on the light, it was to emptiness. No girl sat industriously copying lists. He stepped to the desk she'd used. The lists were nearly finished. Perhaps she had tired of them and gone back to her room.

She hadn't. The barrenness of the room hit him the moment he stepped in.

"Is anything wrong, Dr. Rogers?" Ginger had left another nurse in charge and followed him.

"I'm afraid there is. I left Marge working in my office. She isn't there."

Ginger bit back an unflattering comment. After all, the girl had sounded sincere. Who was she to blame the doctor for allowing his own niece a little more freedom? Marge had seemed so penitent, almost defenseless, sitting there with tears pouring down her face. Quietly, without alerting the rest of the staff, they searched the dormitory, the hospital, even the grove by the doctors' quarters.

"She's been here." Ginger hated having to do it, but she held up a crumpled note. It must have fallen from Marge's pocket when she threw herself at Lee earlier.

Dr. Rogers looked old as he read Lee's note aloud.

"Oh, no!" Ginger's involuntary cry was echoed in Dr. Rogers's face. "The crazy kid! She doesn't know what she's doing! Getting mixed up with anyone who is evidently nothing but trouble. It's only one step above suicide!"

"Where would you go if you were in their shoes? If this place was too hot for you? If they were on the lookout for you in town? If you wanted to pilfer something — and then run off fast?"

Dr. Rogers stared at the tired nurse. Somehow or other they both thought of the Fishing Bridge dispensary.

Fear shut off Ginger's words, but she managed to gasp, "You don't think . . ."

"I don't know. But I'm going to find out." He paused, remembering. "Ginger, get that letter from Misty out of Marge's room. I remember still seeing it there when we checked. I want to know exactly what was in it. I'll call the dispensary while you're gone." He dialed the familiar number. It rang. Once, twice, five times, ten times. No answer.

"Here's the letter." Ginger ran in.

He snatched it up. If only it would give a clue!

Ginger saw the torment in his face and her heart went out to him. What he must be going through!

Dr. Rogers read the letter and left it on the desk. "I doubt if Marge ever read this. If she had, I don't think even she would dare go out and meet Lee as she has evidently done. It spells things out pretty plain."

"What did Misty say on the phone?"

"She didn't answer." Their eyes met in a long gaze.

"That's bad news," Ginger said. "She never goes to bed early and it really isn't light enough for a walk now. I'm going to see if she's all right."

"Not without me." He was moving toward the door when she stopped him.

"Dr. Rogers, our patient — he might need you."

"I have to know if Misty — Miss McCall — is all right!" There was agony in his voice. Yet even as he stood there, she could see him weighing the possibilities. Misty might just have stepped out for a moment. The present patient could very well need him.

It was a terrible decision, choosing duty over checking on the girl he loved. Loved! Even through all his worry the thunderbolt revelation rocked him. So that was it, the reason he had been so furious when she didn't trust him. He loved her. But there was no time now for such thoughts. He and Ginger both had jobs to do.

"Call me the minute you get there," he said.

"I will." She was out the door, running. A moment more and she was back. "Your car's gone, Dr. Rogers!"

He whirled toward her. "Impossible!"

"Does Marge know where you keep your keys?"

He seemed to grow smaller. "Yes, she does."

"Never mind. What now?" But before the words were out of her mouth, Dr. Rogers was hurrying toward the ambulance entrance. "Frank!"

"Yes, sir." Frank had been standing by, not knowing if he would be needed to take the appendectomy patient elsewhere.

"Take Miss Snapp to Fishing Bridge, pronto!"

The Fishing Bridge dispensary was dark and silent when they arrived. Frank had not turned on the siren. If Misty was in danger from a thug, it wouldn't help. It might even work on Lee Crandall's twisted mind to create further havoc. They had been silent on the way over except for Ginger's short explanation.

"You stay here." It was an order, but Ginger ignored him.

Frank grabbed her as her hand was on the door handle. "Ginger, I said for you to stay here and I meant it!"

Without another word he stepped out and walked to the door. There was something evil about that silent dispensary. There should have been lights. Misty never closed up and went to bed at this time of night! Frank knocked, then turned the doorknob. It was locked. Stepping back, he threw the weight of his outdoor-conditioned body against it and fell headlong into the room.

A few hours earlier Misty had been working on some reports when she heard a knock. Then the door opened.

"Why, Marge!" Misty was surprised. The younger girl's face was shining, her eyes bright. "What are you doing here?"

"Just thought I'd stop in and visit a little. Uncle Neil loaned me his car and —"

"Loaned you his car?" Misty's sense of danger had been alerted. Never in the world would Neil have lent this girl his car when she had acted as she had done. Something was wrong. But before Misty could even stand up, a bearded giant stepped in behind Marge and closed the door. His eyes were red-rimmed, reminding Misty of a mad dog she had once faced.

"We'll just take the contents of that, Miss Nursey." He motioned to the locked medication cabinet.

So that was it. Lee Crandall had come back. Somehow Marge had slipped from her watchful guards. How could she?

"Did you read my letter, Marge?" Misty saw in the uncomprehending stare the girl gave her that the letter had not been read. She also saw the blind determination of the girl to help this man, criminal though he might be. *Dear God, what can I do?* An unconscious prayer formed in her heart, a cry for the only help available.

"Can the gossip and get me the keys to that cabinet! And I want anything else that's valuable in this place!" An ugly snub-nosed gun had appeared in Lee Crandall's hand.

Marge stared. "Where did you get that gun?" Something in her voice gave away the truth to Misty. Marge had not expected any violence. She had merely brought him here to get whatever they could.

"I said get me those keys!"

Misty hesitated. If she didn't, he would probably shoot her, smash the cabinet, and take the drugs anyway. It was a pitiful haul, just enough

101

for emergencies. Then he would steal what little money he could find and anything else that took his fancy — though there really wasn't anything here. But he wouldn't know that. Criminals like Lee were often illogical. He was desperate enough to want anything. Her fingers shook as she pushed the keys across the desk to him.

"Good nursey. Now, Marge, you tie her up and gag her!"

Misty started to speak, but the gun waved at her again. Maybe it would be best to submit, but if she did, what would happen to Marge? The girl mustn't go with him. Could she prevent it?

As Marge started toward her, Misty stood and put her arms out as if to be bound. But a moment later she shoved Marge under the desk and threw herself at Lee Crandall. There was a loud explosion. Then all was still. . . .

Somewhere through the pain and blackness Misty could hear voices. Everything seemed hazy, far off, but those voices were there.

"You've killed her!"

"So what? You didn't think I was going to let her get away with that, did you? Now you get over there against that wall. Throw me your scarf."

"What are you doing? You said you loved me. You said we'd go away together."

"You're the one who said all that, baby. You'd be nothing but a drag to me. Thanks for the help!"

A cry broke through Misty's pain, a cry that was suddenly cut off. Evidently the speaker had been stopped. But how? Even through her own horror Misty felt she must get to that speaker, the one who had cried out meaningless sounds. There was a loud thud, then blackness again.

How long was it since everything had grown dark? Misty opened her eyes. Was she blind? No, a crack of light filtered in from somewhere. Her head was throbbing. She reached up to feel the stickiness of blood. How long had she lain there? What had happened? Oh, yes. Marge Crawford and Lee Crandall. Where were they now? A low moan came from somewhere to the right of her. But before Misty could move, the sound of steps outside froze her in place.

"Misty. Misty, are you here?" Someone was rattling the doorknob. It sounded like Frank Jensen — but it couldn't be! What would Frank be doing here? She opened her mouth to call out, but it felt fuzzy. No words would come.

The next moment there was a tremendous crash. Had the dispensary been struck by lightning? Something hit the floor. Then in a moment lights flooded on. It *was* Frank and . . .

"Ginger!"

"Misty, are you all right?" Ginger was kneeling beside her, feeling the lump on her head, stanching the flow of blood, although most of it was dry now.

"Marge? Is she . . . ?" Misty couldn't ask the question.

Frank was bending over the girl with the gag in her mouth, the girl who had been struck down and now lay senseless at his feet. "She's still out, but I don't think she's seriously hurt."

Misty was fast regaining her own wits. "They came. He wanted anything he could get his hands on. . . ." Her voice trailed off. She was so terribly tired. She could hear Ginger at the phone. Whom was she calling?

"We're bringing in Misty and Marge, Dr. Rogers. They're both going to be *all right*." She stressed the words. "We'll be there in just a short time. If we put them both in one room, it will be easier to watch them. . . . No, Misty won't mind."

Misty never remembered the ride from the Fishing Bridge dispensary to the hospital at Lake. She didn't even remember being taken from the ambulance to the room. She was just too tired to care. One thing she did remember. And later she wondered if it was a dream. It was awakening much later, her head aching. Someone was by her bed, ready with a hypodermic needle to give her rest. Was it only imagination, or did someone gently smooth the hair back from her hot face and say, "Sleep well, my darling."

She was too far gone to know. But when she awoke the next morning, it was to see Dr. Rogers asleep in a chair by her bed. She studied him, the dark stubble on his face, the crumpled hospital coat. Had he stayed all night?

Was it Misty's intent gaze that roused the

doctor? He opened his eyes and looked at her a little sheepishly. "Good morning, Misty McCall." But when she tried to answer, he held up his hand. "No talking for a while."

She couldn't keep the question from her eyes. He caught it and looked at her soberly. "Margie's going to be all right. She had a concussion, but she'll be fine in a few days."

"If she'd only read my letter!" It was all he would let Misty say.

Within a few days Misty was up and around. Because of her bad experience at Fishing Bridge, another nurse was going there. There was no danger now. Lee Crandall had been picked up in Dr. Rogers's car as he tried to leave the park. Why he hadn't ditched the car they would never know. Again it was a case of not thinking logically.

Neither Misty nor Marge knew how he'd threatened, "I'll kill those two! Someday I'll get them!"

Lee would be put away for a long time. When the trial was held, both Marge and Misty would have to testify. Until then, he was out of their lives.

Ginger and Misty did everything they could to help Marge, even to calling her Margie. She was pale, subdued. She realized what a fool she had been, how Lee had used her for his own purposes. It had made a tremendous impact on her. Often Misty would find Margie's eyes on her as she busied herself in the room. Then one day the girl said, "I never did read your letter. May I have it now?"

"Of course, Margie." There was no hatred in Misty's tone, only gentleness.

This girl had learned a lesson in a terrible way. How sad that it had to be like that! Yet even so it was better for her to learn now than to be mixed up with people like Lee.

Margie waited until she was alone. She thought of that other day when she had thrown down this letter and kissed the note from Lee. Lee Crandall, her big hero! Her mouth tasted like ashes. All he had ever wanted from her was what she could do for him! A sob tore her throat. Then slowly she picked up the letter and began to read.

Dear Marge,

I felt I should write you just a note to let you know how concerned I am about you. I know you don't care for me at all. That's your privilege. I do hope you'll at least read this letter and try to understand why I've written it.

Marge, your uncle loves you very much. He's always loved you. He wants to see you become the kind of person I know you can be. But getting involved with people like Lee is not the way. Believe me, I know what I'm talking about! I worked with many delinquents in the hospital where I trained. If I could make you see what I had to see! I used to go home at night and be violently sick because of the sad, ruined lives I saw.

Some kids got into trouble at first just because they were bored, or they thought they hated their parents, or they got mixed up with the wrong kind of friends. It was a joke to some of them — at first.

But one crime leads to another. And there's only trouble ahead. I saw kids who were shot, stabbed, beaten to a pulp. I saw a girl like you who was paralyzed for life by a bullet from her boyfriend's gun. A boy like Lee Crandall.

If Lee Crandall is the thug he appears to be, you can't depend on him. He could turn on you in an instant. I've seen cases where that happened. Right now he sees you as useful. When that ends, beware, Marge.

I hope someday we can be friends.

Misty

Margie put down the letter. She felt torn a million ways. Why hadn't she read the letter earlier? It might have stopped so many things. Or would it? She remembered the thrill of meeting Lee, the excitement, the way he kissed her. Would Misty's letter have stopped her then? Probably not. She would have gone to any place in the world he asked her.

Was that love? She hated Lee Crandall now. He had used her. He had never cared for her at all. Had she ever loved him, or was it all infatuation? She closed her eyes, thinking of the way she had seen Frank Jensen look at Ginger. A feeling of envy, of loneliness went through her. Would any man ever look at her that way? With respect? The guys looked at her, all right, but not like that. Her face burned. They looked at her tight jeans and shirts. What would it be like to have someone really care for her as a person, not just a good-time girl?

For the first time in her life Margie Crawford was seeing herself as others saw her. It wasn't pleasant. The way Lee Crandall had shoved her aside, even crashing that gun down on her head, told her more of how cheaply she had held herself than anything else could have done.

Dad and Mom were due in any day now. What would happen to her? A lot of it would depend on Uncle Neil. If the hospital chose to press charges, she was in deep trouble. Who cared? She was in trouble, anyway, enough to last a life-time!

Why hadn't she made more of this chance to come up here? In spite of her trying to attract the males around, Margie had come to really like Yellowstone Park. Now she'd have to leave, to go home, maybe spend years in a correctional school or something.

Hot tears slipped from under the tightly closed eyelids, making tracks of misery down the pale face. If life ever gave her another chance, she'd be pretty careful how she used it, that was for sure!

While she was facing her own actions, Dr. Rogers was discussing her with Ginger and Misty.

"Well, I've failed. I really thought I could help her, up here away from the crowd she ran with. I guess water seeps to its own level. She discovered the lowest of the low when she attached herself to Lee Crandall." His voice was bitter.

"It's been a frightening, cruel experience, but I think she's learned from it," Ginger surprised them by saying. They knew Ginger had never cared for Marge.

"I agree," Misty said. "If only she could stay now that she's gone through it. I think you'd find her a far different girl."

Dr. Rogers stared at the two nurses. "After everything, you still think she deserves another chance?"

"Deserves? No. But I think if she were given that chance, Margie Crawford might surprise us all."

It was food for thought. Long after Dr. Rogers had gone to his quarters that night, he thought of it. Were Misty and Ginger right? Would it be worth his while to see if she could be assigned to his care? What about the upcoming winter, one that would be hectic at best, moving to Mammoth? How would Marge fit in?

For that matter, would Misty even be there? They hadn't spoken of it since the day he had punished her mistrust of him by kissing her so harshly. He shoved back that thought. He had enough on his mind right now. The Crawfords would be there soon. He'd better settle things in his own mind first. No, he couldn't do it. He couldn't take any further responsibility for Margie, even for his sister's sake.

But even as he made his decision, Misty's face floated before him. Her words haunted him. "Deserves? No. But I think if she were given that chance . . ."

It brought on a sleepless night. He had to face it. With her wisdom, if Misty thought Margie was worth it, he'd give her that chance.

Chapter 8

It was a subdued Margie Crawford who walked the hospital halls, doing her maid's work as she should have done it before. Her parents had come. She had been taken to Helena. No one but Neil and her parents knew what had transpired.

All Neil told Ginger and Misty was, "She is assigned to my care for the rest of the summer. After that —" His expressive shrug only hinted at the future.

With the new attitude in Margie, things moved more smoothly. As if to make up for the slack spell during all the rain, patients came in hordes, transported from all parts of the park.

One horrendous case Misty would never forget. She had regained her strength completely and was due to go on night duty with Ginger. But about five o'clock that fateful afternoon, Dr. Rogers sent for them both. "I'm going to need some extra help. Frank's bringing in a badly hurt man. He was mangled by a bear."

"Oh, no!" Ginger's face turned white.

And Misty said, "I didn't think we had bear problems since they drove the grizzlies back in the woods."

"We don't, normally. But this man insisted on going off the marked trails. He was with a guided trip, but it wasn't enough. He disappeared from the rest of the group early this morning, taking his sleeping bag with him. I guess he intended to camp out on his own. There are always a few who will not obey rules! The guide knew there were grizzlies in the forest. He tracked the man. When he got there, he was second on the scene. A bear had already tangled with him. From what the guide says, the tourist must have been cooking bacon. I suppose he is ignorant of wild animals, but it appears the bear came, grabbed for the bacon, and the man tried to stop him. It enraged the bear. If the tourist hadn't been wearing a heavy mackinaw, he would have been killed. As it is, he's just about shredded to ribbons with bear scratches and has lost a lot of blood."

No matter how long she lived, Misty would never forget the sight of that particular patient when he was brought in. It took all her training to keep from turning and running. It was true. He had been clawed terribly. They could only guess how far he'd crawled, or how long it had been until the guide found him. He had fainted on the way in in the ambulance, thank God! The pain must have been great.

It took a long time to clean, suture, and dress those wounds. Hands, arm, face, legs, torso — there was scarcely any part of his body that hadn't been clawed, except his left arm. He must have kept it back. It took several transfusions to bring any degree of color back to the pale face.

He wasn't a young man. He was middle-aged,

old enough to know better than to disobey park rules. He would carry scars the rest of his life from his little encounter.

"I'm still uncertain why Dr. Rogers asked us to help. The afternoon nurses are great," Misty said.

Ginger looked at her friend. "Maybe he wants you to get an idea of what this winter's cases will be like. The animals come down during the winter. Sometimes two and three hundred starving elk will be down around Mammoth. They're thick. There are also lots of coyotes. They're cowardly and don't attack. But remember one thing, Misty. If an animal gets hungry enough or frightened enough, he will get food any way he can. Today's incident was from human stupidity. Our winter accidents are not necessarily that. We have only a few wolves, no cougars. But an elk will charge sometimes."

Misty shivered. "I guess people just don't realize how dangerous wild animals can be."

Ginger's face was sober. "That's the whole trouble. They are wild animals, not tame kitty cats or dogs to play with. Another thing humans do is to upset nature's balance. In so many parts of the country open season has been declared against cougars."

"But shouldn't the cougars be destroyed? They kill deer and elk!"

"That's right, and it seems cruel. But is it any more cruel than thousands of animals starving to death because of lack of food?"

At Misty's shocked look, Ginger explained. "I remember not too many years ago there were a lot of cougars in the Grand Canyon area in Arizona. They were killing off the deer. Open season was declared and many of the cougars were killed, leaving only a few. Within a few years, there were so many thousands of deer around the Grand Canyon, there was not enough left for them to eat. One winter they counted thousands of dead deer. They had starved."

"Nature is terrible!"

"No." Ginger looked at Misty with the wisdom of the earth in her eyes. "Cougars thin out the deer and elk herds, it's true. But they take as a general rule the weak, the sick, those that are a drag on the herd. They also provide a natural balance. I can't fault them for that. When man steps in out of kindness for the poor deer, or elk, he upsets that balance and there is starvation."

"It seems so cruel."

"In some ways it is. Survival of the fittest. Yet don't we see the same thing in people, Misty? We can get two patients with the same illness, the same chance of recovery. One lives, one dies, although each receives equal care. Why? I've come to feel it's the will to survive." Ginger paused, looking out the window. "Everything in nature is created for a purpose."

"Even those?" Misty pointed a distasteful finger at an ugly black bird flying past. She hated them, those buzzards.

"Of course. They're the garbagemen of the animal kingdom. We despise them because they eat carrion. Yet if they didn't, what would happen? The forests and fields would be left strewn with dead animals. Even the buzzards have their place."

That night, long after Ginger had fallen asleep, Misty was wide-eyed. She was learning so much! What would the coming winter bring? Or would she even be there? Dr. Rogers had said nothing more about the job. Perhaps he wouldn't want a nurse who hadn't trusted him. She would have to open the subject, much as she hated to do it. If she wasn't going to stay in the park, she'd better start writing some letters and find a job. Summer was moving along.

Then all at once, it was August 25th.

"Merry Christmas, Misty!" Dr. Rogers laughed at her expression.

"Christmas? What's happening?" Misty had been gone for a few days' vacation. She had chosen to visit the Grand Teton Mountains, staying at a guest ranch. Because of it she had missed all the preparations for "Christmas in August."

"Sorry, Misty," said Ginger, who stood next to the doctor. "I guess I forgot to tell you, with all the other excitement and so forth."

Neil broke in. "Miss McCall, for your enlightenment and edification, may I inform you August 25th is *always* Christmas in Yellowstone Park. Behold." He waved to the decorations in the dining room. "It's for all the employees of the park. The Yellowstone Park Company, that is. There are gifts for all. There are buses. To Lower Mammoth. Gardiner. There are big houses, open, welcoming. There are delicacies — ham, turkey, cider. There are Christmas carols —"

"Stop!" Misty was weak from laughing. "Is he kidding?"

"Absolutely not," Ginger assured her. "It's all true."

"I can't believe it!"

But later in the day Misty had to believe it. Christmas in August. The park visitors looked on and laughed. The park employees had a ball. Everything Dr. Rogers had promised was there, and more. Never had Misty enjoyed herself so much. Another doctor was in charge of the hospital that day, leaving Dr. Rogers free to take the two nurses, Frank, and Margie to the celebration.

At the last minute Ginger whispered to Dr. Rogers, "Why don't you ask Jim Robinson along? Margie might feel more comfortable if the number was even."

Neil shot a look at her. "That playboy?"

But later even he had to admit the maintenance man from the hospital added a lot to the day. Jim never let on he had heard a word about Margie. Instead, he made a special effort to be at her side and even succeeded in coaxing a smile or two out of her. She didn't wear the tight clothes she'd affected earlier in the summer. She had on a simple pants-and-shirt outfit and looked nice. When she saw the look in Jim Robinson's eyes, some of the ice inside that had been there for such a long time began to melt. And by the time they got back, she was a far happier girl than she had been before.

Misty noticed the seemingly mutual attraction between the two. She hadn't seen Neil Rogers watching her until he spoke, too low for the others to hear. "Don't let her snitch your boyfriend."

"He's not my boyfriend!" Misty spun around, wearing high flags of color in her face.

"Good." She couldn't help but see the satisfaction in his face. "Besides, don't forget — I asked first."

Of all the infuriating men! Before Misty could think up a sufficiently cutting reply, he had laughed and squeezed her hand. "Don't get mad at me on Christmas, Misty. It's time to sing carols."

Carols sung in August! The very novelty of it would have charmed Misty even if the beauty of the carols hadn't done the trick. As she sang, memories of family Christmases came back. And her feelings showed in her face.

Neil whispered, "Don't look back with sadness, Misty. Remember the good times, but don't let tears drown out the memories."

Misty was grateful for the hard clasp of Neil Rogers's hand. She wouldn't have expected such understanding from him. The warm rush of love for this tall man at her side brought new tears. Would he ever learn to care for her? Would she even be around this winter?

Neil deliberately loosened his hold. "We have a winter Christmas celebration, too, you know. There will be snowmobiling and all kinds of good stuff. We may get snowed in. There will be just a few of us left, then. The Mammoth Inn houses the employees, but you'll have your little log cabin."

Misty swallowed hard, her heart beating fast. "Then — then you still want me?"

"Want you!" Something leaped into the man's eyes. Misty felt her heart rush out to meet it, but he only laughed. "You don't think I'm going to let a good nurse like you get away, do you?"

A moment later he was gone. He was chatting with Frank, leaving Misty staring after him. How silly she had been to think he might care. All he wanted was a good nurse. Well, that's what he'd get. Unconsciously her chin squared. If she couldn't win his love, at least she'd win his admiration and respect as a nurse.

If Misty could have known the thoughts churning inside Neil Rogers at that moment, she wouldn't have seen her future in quite the same way. For one moment he had been tempted to hold her close, tell her just how much he wanted her. No, he had done that once, punishing her for her lack of faith. Never again, not like that.

Someday he would tell her he cared. Not yet.

She might turn to him in gratefulness. He wanted her love, the love she would give to only one man. He wanted her forever — his wife, companion, helper, mother of his children. At that point he cut off his daydream. Time enough for that later.

There was a biding-my-time look in Dr. Rogers's face as he drove home. Misty was quiet beside him, Margie on her other side. Jim and Frank were mildly arguing in the back seat, a drowsy Ginger between them.

Suddenly they were electrified by Neil's asking, "Margie, would you like to spend the winter with me in Upper Mammoth?"

The girl gasped. Had he read her mind? This day had taught her what fun, what a wonderful time, she could have doing simple things. She had found for the first time the simple joy of being together with those who liked her. If only she could keep it up!

"You — you mean stay on working for the park?"

"That's not exactly what I had in mind. I was wondering if you'd like to run my home for me." Only Misty caught the grin in his voice as he added casually, "I had someone else in mind, but it didn't work out."

Misty's gasp was lost in Margie's answer. "I'd love it. But what would I have to do?"

Misty barely heard Dr. Rogers's reply. How could he refer to that insane proposal? What if someone else caught on?

"Oh, cooking, dishes, housework. All that. I'll be keeping a bachelor hall, you know. Think you could handle it?"

Even through her own preoccupation, Misty noticed the uncertainty of Margie's reply. The girl had been so brash, so sure of her own ability to do everything in the world, it seemed strange to hear her falter, "I'd try."

"Good. I've already asked your folks. They said fine."

"Hey, Margie," Jim said. "I'm putting my bid in early. Will you come up to college for our Winter Carnival?"

Again Misty was struck by the new humility in the girl's voice. Instead of casually tossing off something, she asked, "May I, Neil?"

"We'll see if you're a good girl between now and then."

A groan came from the back seat. Jim complained, "Oh, great. Now he's going to play the heavy parent. I'll have to get in good with this guy if I'm going to date you, Margie!"

This time it was Margie who gasped. She had thought Jim was only being polite as her day's escort.

Impulsively Misty reached over and touched the younger girl's hand. She was surprised to feel the cold fingers curl around her own. Why, in many ways Margie was still a child! There was something hesitant, confiding in the way she had reached out and taken the offered hand. And Misty thought: *I can do some real missionary work with this girl. I can get to know her and maybe give her some better deals than she has, and* . . . Misty laughed at herself. Trust her to think up some big project. She'd be busy enough fitting into the winter way of life in her new job and her log cabin!

The next few weeks passed incredibly fast. Before Misty was aware of it, summer was replaced by the gloriously colored fall. The hospital closed in mid-September. Misty felt sad the last time she saw it. But her heart also swelled. Here had been her first job, her first triumphs and failures. Would she be back next year? Or would she stay on at Mammoth?

The leaves of gold and orange crunched underfoot. The dark green evergreens pointed the way to heaven and the bluest sky in the world. Snow appeared like magic on the tops of the highest peaks. But Misty didn't care. She was snugly moved into her log cabin. It was a primitive place, but attractive. Ginger and Margie had helped her make red-print curtains for the windows. She also made a curtain to cover the area that served as a closet at the end of the tiny bedroom. The main room barely held a shabby couch, one chair, and the monstrous woodburning stove that both provided heat and served for cooking.

Misty had gasped at that stove. "Cook, on that — that *thing?*"

"Sure. You'll be fine. There's stacks and stacks

of wood behind the cabin. Good and dry, too. You'll be snug here." Dr. Rogers caught sight of her downcast face and relented. "I'll lend you a portable electric heater and a hot plate to use until you get used to the stove."

It really hadn't taken so long. Misty curled up in satisfaction now, watching the red glow of flames through the tiny windows. Her approving gaze took in the afghan over her knees, compliments of the departing doctor and his wife. Its oranges, reds, and golds blended with the plain brown slipcovers Misty had selected for couch and chair to hide their worn condition. While the floor was only linoleum, it had been waxed to a high shine, its scuffed spots hidden by strategically placed braided rugs.

This is happiness. Misty stretched, surprised by a knock at the door. Her first visitors?

"Come in!"

Dr. Rogers and Margie stepped inside. Margie had really helped get Misty settled, but it was the first time Neil had been in the little log cabin since they had finished.

"What a homey little nest!" he said.

"Just like a honeymoon cottage." Misty's words slipped out. She bit her lip, wishing she could recall them. But Neil only laughed and didn't comment. His heart was already doing tricks at the sight of Misty curled up in a warm housecoat. He was used to seeing her in uniform or slacks.

"If I ever get married I wouldn't care if I didn't

ever live in any better place than this." Margie's wistful voice broke into Misty's consciousness.

"It is nice, isn't it?" She led the way to the spotless bedroom and the minuscule bath. "The shower is so small I can barely turn around, but at least I have indoor plumbing!" She and Ginger had painted the walls green and hung up a pretty shower curtain. They had also put a rug on the floor.

"These floors can be icy in winter. You'll want something warm to step out on," Ginger had warned.

"I guess what I really like best is that it's mine — at least for the winter. I paid the rent until next May. It's going to seem strange living in my own little house. For the last several years it's been a dormitory room, usually with a room-mate. I didn't realize until I came here how nice it would be to have a place of my own." She smiled at Margie. "Maybe someday you will have a place like it."

"I hope so. Neil will get married and there won't be a place for me." But Margie didn't look downcast at the prospect. "Who knows? I might marry a park employee and live right here my-self!"

Neil didn't catch the laughing exchange of glances between the two girls. In the short time since they'd come to Upper Mammoth they had become friends. Ginger came over as often as she could from Gardiner, but it was Margie who had been right there all the time. They had helped each other settle in.

Margie had laughed at herself. "Guess I was just a frustrated homemaker and didn't know it. I wouldn't tell Uncle Neil for the world, but I absolutely love puttering around, fixing up messes for his dinner, trying new recipes." She wrinkled her nose. "I even like cleaning, seeing how shining everything can be! Although I haven't had to do much of that. The doctor's wife even waxed the floors before she left!"

The more Misty spent time with the younger girl, the more she realized the potential within her. Since she'd left off the tight clothing and heavy makeup, her own natural good looks were starting to shine through. It was more than that, though. Margie really felt responsible, needed. Hadn't she been given duties at home? Misty never asked. But here with a whole house as her job, Margie really came through. She also proved invaluable in other ways. When Misty was busy helping Neil, Margie sometimes served as their receptionist. Again, she did a good job. She was learning to smile, to create confidence in a waiting patient. Who knew? Maybe someday she would want to get training for something, perhaps even in the medical field. For now it was enough that she was happy and busy.

The only disruption in those first few months was when they had to testify against Lee Crandall. The hospital had dropped the charges against Margie for her pilfering, but Lee's theft and vicious attack on Misty at the Fishing Bridge dispensary were another matter. So was his taking Neil's car and trying to escape.

The trial was a horror. Margie reverted to a frightened child and clung to Misty. But when she had to testify, she did it honestly. She told everything — how they had gone to the dispensary, how she hadn't known he was going to hurt Misty, how he had knocked her out, then turned on Margie herself.

"I'll get you, you —" Lee's pulled-back lips were menacing.

But he was cut off by the judge's curt words. "You won't be hurting anyone where you're going."

White and spent, Margie sobbed as they got back in the car. "How could I ever have thought I . . . I cared for that creep?"

Neil reached over to hug her. "It's all over, Margie. Do you hear me? It's all over. What counts is what happens from here on out."

But it was a miserable girl who cried herself to sleep that night. The whole story would be in the papers. What would people think of her? Margie couldn't admit, even to herself, her fear of what "people" would think really narrowed itself down to Jim Robinson.

Chapter 9

Misty's eyes as well as her cheeks glowed as she ran the short distance from her log cabin to Dr. Rogers's office. The frost had been so thick when she awakened, for a minute she wondered if an early snow had come. It was a sparkling world, a study in contrasts. She filled her lungs with the clean, cold air, drinking in the blue sky, piles of golden leaves, white-capped peaks, and fading red streaks of sunrise.

Oh, oh. She had learned to take seriously the old saw, "Red sky in the morning, sailor take warning." There had been one or two storms since she came, always following a gloriously alive sunrise such as the one surrounding her now.

There was a smile on her lips, a snatch of song under her breath, as she burst into the office.

Neil Rogers looked up, noting what a picture she made in her warm parka, eyes alight with the joy of living. "Someone's happy."

His small nurse grinned back. Misty had learned to know him well during the short time they'd been at Mammoth. She had admired and respected him when she worked with him at Lake. She had even begun to fall in love with him, been disillusioned about Margie, then had her faith restored. All of it was nothing compared to the feelings he generated in her now. In their work she saw him at his best and worst. Both were magnificent. When it came to carelessness that produced accidents and hurt people, his eyes turned glacial. They could bore right through a parent who didn't watch children, or someone who didn't take care of himself.

Misty had learned Dr. Rogers's favorite expression was, "God gave you one body. You'd better take care of it." Often he pointed out the window to a spanking clean car. "If you'd put as much time into taking care of your body as you do your car I'd be out of business."

He was stern but just. He was also tender, kind, loving. She had seen small children crow in delight when he played with them. What a father he would make! Sometimes Misty visualized him in his house, not with Margie as his housekeeper, but with a wife. But the face wouldn't come clear. She didn't want it to.

She had always thought girls who proclaimed to the world, "I'll die if he doesn't love me," the stupidest girls on earth. Now she had compassion for them. Her own traitorous heart told her much of life's brightness would fade if Neil couldn't ever care for her.

So she waited, working with him, learning to know him. She also learned to know Margie better. Many conversations were held in the cozy log cabin with the red-print curtains.

"I never knew how good it felt to rest." Margie stretched her tired muscles one evening. "I swear. Never again will I think of anyone as 'just a housewife.' Why, you have to be plumber, electrician, chef, janitor, and who knows what else!" She smiled. "Misty, I wouldn't have confessed this earlier, but I still love it."

"Good practical training for your future."

Margie sat up with a jerk. "My future?"

"Sure. Didn't you say you wanted to get married and live in a log cabin like mine? Of course, when kids come along, you'd have to make it bigger, and —" Her words were cut off with a carefully aimed pillow from Margie.

"Seriously, have you thought about what you'd like to do?" Misty asked.

Margie was silent a long time, staring at the little windows in the stove, seeing the red flames dancing behind them. "I'd like to be useful. For a long time I felt the world was so rotten there was no use doing anything. Now I see that it won't be a better place unless I help make it better. I'd like to be like you and Ginger and Dr. Rogers, I mean Uncle Neil, and Frank, and — and Jim Robinson."

"He's been writing to you, hasn't he?"

"Yes." The girl's face was in partial shadow.

Misty kept her voice light. "Good! You know Jim will be through with college this year. Has he decided what he's going to do?"

Margie lost her reticence. "He sure has. You know he's taking the courses necessary for a park ranger/naturalist the same as Frank. Well, both their applications have been approved. They will be right here in Yellowstone Park next summer!"

Before she could keep back the words, Misty said, "You'll like that, won't you, Margie?"

"Yes." The answer was muffled. "But I keep thinking how awful it was, the way I acted when I first came, and Lee Crandall and everything. You know Jim flirted with me then. I can't help but wonder if he still thinks I'm the same kind of girl."

"I doubt that. He flirted with every girl, even me when I first came. But in a nice way. He had no intention of getting entangled." She saw the droop to Margie's lips. "I wouldn't tell you this if I didn't really mean it. You are the first girl Jim has ever kept in contact with after the summer season was over. Or so I understand. Always before he dated, then he let them go. But Frank told Ginger Jim hasn't dated anyone since he got back to college. He's really anxious for us to go up for the Ice Carnival."

There was a rush of flying feet. Then two arms hugged Misty hard. "You'll never know how much I needed to hear that! But why hasn't Jim said anything more serious in his letters?"

Misty hated to do it but Margie had matured. She could probably handle the truth. "I think he's giving you time to grow up, honey." She could feel tension in the girl. "He knows you've gone through a pretty shattering summer all around. You need time. He wouldn't want a girl on the rebound. Jim's older. He knows what he wants, and if Frank is right, you're it. You'll have to prove to him you're worth it."

"Thanks, Misty." Margie's voice was husky. "I deserved that. But don't think I can't do it — I can! By the time he graduates next spring, Mr. Jim Robinson is going to find an entirely different girl from the one he knew this summer!" She laughed, then turned red. "Don't you think June would be a nice time for a honeymoon — with a brand new ranger/naturalist?"

"It would be a nice time for a honeymoon." Misty's heart added, *with a doctor who has taken over a practice in Mammoth.* But Margie couldn't read minds, fortunately! Or could she?

"Misty." Her tone was hesitant. "I don't want to butt in or be rude or anything, but there's something I think you should know."

What was there in her simple statement to set Misty's heart beating hard? "What's that?"

"Well, I know Uncle Neil likes you a lot and everything. I'd have to be blind not to see it. I think you like him, too." She paused, but Misty was mute. "I wouldn't want you to get hurt, or anything. I've even prayed you two would get together." She was so earnest Misty didn't have the heart to reprove her. Besides, hadn't she prayed the same thing, not in words, but with her heart?

"He carries a picture of some girl in his wallet. I wasn't snooping, but he gave me some money to get groceries and I caught a tiny glimpse of a picture. It was of him and a girl. Before I could even see if I knew her, he saw me looking at his wallet and snapped it shut and shoved it back in

130

his pocket. Like I said, I didn't even get a good look. He never said a word, but his face kind of closed up, if you know what I mean."

Misty knew what she meant. Her own face felt closed up. So there was another girl. But where was she? There had been no evidence of any girl all summer or fall. She used every bit of dramatic ability she had to laugh. "It would be unnatural for him not to have a girl, Margie."

She must have been successful because Margie just looked at her and said, "But I wanted it to be you."

What if Margie carried the thought to Neil? What if he were to feel sorry for her, think she had taken seriously that ridiculous proposal made so long ago and his laughing reference to it later? Misty didn't want that to happen. So, without thinking, she said, "That would be a bit awkward. You see, I'm planning to be married."

If Margie hadn't been so thunderstruck she would have caught Misty's quick intake of breath. Misty wondered at her own strange words. It's not a lie, her conscience soothed. After all, you do plan to be married someday, don't you?

"Married! Does Uncle Neil know?"

"No. There's no date set. I'd rather you didn't say anything to him, or anyone." *She'd better not. If she does, where can I produce even a reasonable facsimile of a fiancé?* Misty giggled nervously. "It won't interfere with my work this winter, so I'd rather just not say anything about it, keep it a secret."

If Misty hadn't been so involved in her involuntary and monstrous deception, she would have seen the long, level look Margie gave her. There was something fishy about all this. Where was this fiancé, if Misty planned to get married? Margie smiled to herself.

"Sure, Misty. You keep my secret, I'll keep yours."

But on the way back to the doctor's house Margie thought of Misty's obvious embarrassment once she had made her little statement. Misty didn't have any fiancé. She had only said that because of what Margie had said about the picture.

Margie's mind was devious enough to add: *Then if she doesn't have any secret, you won't be breaking your word if you mention it, will you?* She had found out what she wanted to know, although it was true about the picture. Now she would see what she could find out from Neil.

Margie timed her comments perfectly.

The next evening he came in smiling. "I've never had a nurse I could work with so perfectly as Miss McCall. She's super. We certainly make a good team. She anticipates my every need."

She does, does she? Margie was casual. "It's too bad she probably won't be here after this year."

Neil put down the fork he had been using to attack Margie's lasagna. It was good and he was hungry, or had been. "She won't? Why not?"

Margie's face was innocent. "She told me she

planned to be married. She didn't say when, but any man would be stupid not to marry her as soon as he could, so I guessed maybe they'd get married next summer."

Neil's fork pushed the lasagna around his plate. Margie's keen eyes took it all in. "Did she say who it was?" he asked.

"No. I thought maybe you knew."

This time the fork speared viciously. "I do not."

"Then maybe I shouldn't have said anything. She didn't want to discuss it, but since you work so closely I was sure you'd know about it."

Neil stood up. "Sorry, Margie. I have to rush. There's a bunch of paperwork that has to be finished tonight." He was gone before she could reply.

Margie sat at the table eyeing his half-eaten dinner with satisfaction. It was a small price to have paid for learning what she had learned!

A few days later Misty asked Dr. Rogers, "Is there anything wrong? You seem a little preoccupied these days."

So it showed that much. Neil wouldn't for the world tell her what was wrong. He couldn't say, "I hoped all the time you'd learn to know and love me. Now I find out you are engaged, have been this whole time. Why didn't you tell me, before I made a fool of myself and fell in love?"

Instead he said, "There is something about that new patient that bothers me. Have you ever seen him before?"

It instantly wiped out Misty's former question. "No, I don't think so, but I get the feeling I know him." She shivered. "I even get the feeling he knows me, or has known me at some time. The way he looks at me when I'm in the room gives me the creeps. And when Margie came in the other day he glared at her as if he hated her. Maybe he just hates women."

"I don't think so. But I'll be glad when that wound heals and he doesn't come in for dressings anymore." There was more truth in that than Dr. Rogers cared to state. From the time Van Jones came in with a profusely bleeding hand, compliments of an axe wound, there had been something about him Neil didn't like.

It had been more than the matted, dirty hair tied back with a string, or the wild look in his eye. His language had been so rotten Neil had told him, "Knock it off! We've got people around here who don't have to listen to that!"

The fanatical glare had turned on him, then Misty, but he had at least shut up. In the succeeding visits he'd kept still, but he still glared at them.

Misty had been right. When Margie had been acting as receptionist the other day, the Jones character had literally stared her down.

"Did you ask Margie if she knew him?" Misty dreaded to ask the question. She needn't have.

"She doesn't know him. She's just like us. He looks familiar but isn't anyone she can recognize."

"Well, after this next week he will be out of our hair."

Neil's answer was slow, deliberate. "I'm not too sure of that. I saw him going into that log cabin across from yours. I think he's rented it." He abruptly changed the subject. "You always lock your door at night, don't you, Misty?"

She looked up in surprise. "Of course. I feel silly doing it, with virtually no trouble here, but I always do before I go to sleep."

"Good. You never know what kind of creeps may be around."

Was he referring to Van Jones? She thought of it that night as she closed the door behind her, securing the heavy bolt. A few minutes later she heard crunchy footsteps, slow, a bit muffled. There was nothing unusual in that. Many people went past her little cabin. What was unusual was the deliberateness of them, the almost furtive way they stopped and started.

She slipped to her tiny bedroom, being careful not to turn on a light, and peered from the window. Nothing there. Must have been her imagination. But when she got back to the couch and picked up a book, she involuntarily glanced at the door. There was no imagining what she saw. The knob was turning!

Thank God for that sturdy bolt! "Who's there?"

The voice started out as a demand came out as a whisper. It wouldn't have carried across the room, let alone through the heavy logs forming her cabin walls.

Even as she watched, the knob slid back in place. She heard footsteps crossing the tiny porch. Freeing herself from her frozen state, she switched off the lights and tiptoed to the window. She parted the curtains an inch and looked out. The moon had just come out, spilling its light on the earth below. In its beams she saw him — a big, long-haired figure. He crossed the road and opened the door to a log cabin, the cabin Neil said had been rented to "the creep."

Van Jones! What had he wanted? He was several years younger than she. Surely he wasn't after Misty. Then why had he tried the door? If his hand had been hurting and he wanted something, the doctor's office and home were nearly as close.

Misty couldn't ever remember being so frightened. To have that hulking creature try her door. If only she knew why, she could face up to it and do something! She didn't. Again that vague familiarity haunted her. She could almost think who it was he resembled, but not quite. It teased the edge of her consciousness, but refused to materialize.

If only she had a phone! It hadn't seemed necessary. She was so close to the office and doctor's house. Now she would have given anything in the world to call Neil. Should she chance it, bundle up and run to him? No. She couldn't. She didn't have the courage. If Van Jones really were after her, he'd be watching. He could overtake her before she got away from her own little yard. It was late enough so that no one was around. She had to stay there.

All night long Misty sat huddled, watching the doorknob with hypnotic fascination, starting at every little noise outside. Something brushed against the house and she almost panicked. If ever she lived through this night it would be a miracle. Could people die from sheer fright? She had always considered herself courageously in-clined, but not now. That mysterious warning signal at the edge of her mind was enough to keep her upset.

Misty was not smiling or singing when she ar-rived at work the next morning. The sleepless night had taken the starch out of her backbone.

"Misty! What's wrong?" Margie at the recep-tionist desk was on her feet, but no quicker than Neil. He had heard her come in and at Margie's shocked question he was in the outer office.

"Van Jones. He tried to get in my house last night."

Never had Neil seen Misty look as she now did. His blood rose to the boiling point. "That creep! Are you sure it was him?"

"Yes." It was barely a whisper. "Just before bedtime. I locked the door and shot home the bolt as you told me. I heard footsteps, looked out my bedroom window. There was nothing there. I went back in the other room. The doorknob turned. Then it slowly turned back. When I heard footsteps again I turned out the light and ran to the window. It was Van Jones. He was going into his house."

The door to the office slowly opened. None of them heard it. It wasn't until a deep voice spoke that they realized someone had come in. Van Jones stood in the doorway.

Misty shrank back from him and Dr. Rogers demanded, "What are you doing here now? We aren't open yet."

There was a gloating smile with false apology as the bearded man turned to Misty. "I just wanted to apologize to Miss McCall for scaring her. I heard what she said. It's true. All I wanted was something to make me sleep. I thought she might have some sleeping tablets, or something."

"Why didn't you come here, or at least knock?" There was the lash of anger in Neil's question.

It didn't even pierce the outside crust of the man's ego. "Didn't want to bother you. When I got there I just thought maybe it was too late so I tried the door. I went right back to my cabin afterward. Sorry, ma'am." His grin displayed a broken front tooth. "I'm leaving this morning, but I didn't want anyone to be troubled on my account." He turned and stepped out. His backpack was loaded. It was obvious he had been truthful about one thing, at least. He was leaving.

Neil took one step toward the door, but Misty stopped him. "Let him go. We can't prove anything. After all, all he did was try the door."

"You're right. But I can't say I'm not glad to see the last of that creep!"

Margie had been standing wide-eyed. "Me, too. He kind of reminds me of Lee Crandall." She shivered. "How could I ever have thought I liked anyone like that?" Her question wasn't to be answered.

One of the maids from Mammoth Inn came in just then. She had burned her hand on hot water from the tap. Their day had begun.

"Would you like Margie to stay with you tonight? She could sleep on the couch," Neil said during a lull.

Misty gave him a relieved sigh. "I guess I'm an awful coward, but I really would like company, just for tonight. If Van's gone, then there's no danger, but it would be nice to have her."

However, before the day was out, plans had to be changed.

Neil received a call and came back, his face troubled. "There's been a snowmobile accident over toward Dunraven Pass. We're the closest medical help. I'll have to go."

"Do you need me?"

"No. I'd rather you stayed here. I may be gone overnight. I was just wondering — would you rather come up and stay in my place with Margie? I think I'd like to know you were here with a phone, just in case you get scared."

"If that's what you want, it will be fine. I'll pack a bag and be back soon." True to her word, by the time Neil was ready to leave, Misty was back with Margie.

"How do you get there?" Misty asked him.

"Drive as far as I can, then snowmobile. The caller said he'd have one waiting. Dunraven is so high they always get snow sooner than we do." His face wrinkled. "Funny thing, he didn't say how he got word. Must have come in on CB radio or something."

Neil thought again of the odd call when he reached the point where he was to meet the snowmobile. There was no one there. There hadn't been anyone there, either. As far ahead as he could see, there was unbroken snow. Why had he been called? He waited an hour, alternately warming the jeep, then waiting. Finally he gave up and decided to go back. Obviously no one was coming.

He didn't like the looks of this. Why would someone call, then not show? Had he fallen for the oldest trick in the book, a false cry for help? Was he still enough of a park tenderfoot to be tricked? If so, again, why?

Like a light from a beacon came a voice in his mind. Margie, shivering, saying, "He kind of reminds me of Lee Crandall." It couldn't be true. The face was not the same. And Lee Crandall was behind bars. Wasn't he? Yet the more Neil thought of the connection, the more similarities he remembered. The same look in their eyes. The same general messiness. Why hadn't he caught it sooner?

What if this Van Jones were related to Lee? What if family loyalty mingled with madness had caused him to seek out those who had put Lee where he now was?

The sun had long since dropped behind a wall of approaching storm front. He was in for it. But he had to get back. Van Jones had said he was leaving. Had it been true, or only a ruse to disarm their suspicions? He must get back to Mammoth immediately. But how? Even now the snow had started pouring down, hitting the windshield with the force of stinging, biting pellets. Winter had come to Yellowstone Park in earnest, the first big storm of the season. If he had not been so worried, Neil would have enjoyed it. He always liked pitting his strength against the elements, wildly relating to the storms. Not tonight. He would have given everything he possessed to be back at Mammoth.

It was then he decided. If and when this was all over he was going to have it out with Misty, find out who this long-lost fiancé might be. He would fight any man on earth to win her, use the weapons at hand — his need, his reliance on her skill as a nurse, but even more, her loyalty and love as a woman. But it might be a long time in the future. The snow was thickening. He could barely see to drive. Even the faithful jeep would be slowed down.

The hours crawled by, almost as slowly as the jeep. It was long after midnight when an exhausted Neil Rogers drove into Mammoth.

Misty's cabin was dark, silent. It would be, of course. She was with Margie. Everything looked all right at the office. His home was picturesque when outlined by the jeep's headlights. Snow mantled the roof, crowned the dark trees.

He opened the door. Perhaps he had been foolish with all his fears and imaginings. He stopped by Margie's door, tapped gently. No reply. He pushed it open, switched on the light. The bed was smooth. It had not been slept in.

Crowding back his fears he moved on to the guest room. With the storm and everything, maybe Margie had chosen to stay with Misty. There were twin beds in the guest room. Funny, the door stood open. His heart jumped to his throat. No effort now to keep his voice down. "Margie! Misty!" There was no answer. He turned on the lights. The twin beds stood in mute testimony of former occupants. Sheets and blankets were thrown back. A pillow was on the floor. But no one was there.

Racing from room to room, Neil found no further evidence of the two girls. They were gone, as mysteriously as snow vanished before the sun. Then he found it. A kitchen window, forced open. One muddy footprint, melted snow still sloppily staining the floor. It was a large footprint. Van Jones was a big man.

In desperation Neil tore back to Margie's room. He jerked open the closet door. All of Margie's clothes seemed to be there, except her parka. And her boots were missing from the corner where they usually stood. He ran to the guest room. Misty's overnight case stood there. Flannel pajamas and robe were thrown on top of it. Evidently she had on outdoor clothing, too. Because there was none in the room.

Neil stared like a man gone berserk, then rushed to the window. The snow had steadied to large, fluffy flakes. Any trace of a trail would be obliterated within minutes, and the girls had been gone for some time. Snow had blown in through the kitchen window. The beds were cold.

For one moment the world turned black. But Dr. Neil Rogers was not a man to give up. He had struggled for everything worthwhile in life. He would not give up now. Somewhere out in that storm his niece and the woman he loved more than life itself were prisoners of a madman. He was firmly convinced of it. The hours spent in getting back to Mammoth had stamped that feeling indelibly in his mind.

He clenched his hands, those hands that could incise so cleanly, probe, cleanse, and bandage so tenderly. For one moment he wished he had Van Jones in their grip. He would squeeze and squeeze until he forced the truth from that broken-toothed mouth. For the first time in his life Dr. Rogers felt he could kill another human being. He who was dedicated to life could annihilate that creep as easily as he would swat a fly. If anything happened to Margie or Misty, he would track down the man if it took the rest of his life.

Chapter 10

Neil Rogers waited impatiently as the park ranger carefully blotted up the snowy footprint from the kitchen floor. His nerves screamed to be doing something, anything. Out in that storm were two people he loved. An odd little smile crossed his tense features. He hadn't realized until now how very much he had come to love Margie in the weeks since they had moved to Mammoth. The shining clean house showed more clearly than words her struggle to be useful.

"It seems strange to have a park ranger investigating a break-in and kidnapping," Neil said.

The tall man opposite him straightened. Parker Wilson's keen eyes met the doctor's. They were a sharp contrast to his drawling speech. "That's the way we have to run it here. Yellowstone Park isn't under state jurisdiction. It's federal. We take care of what happens. If it gets too big for us, we import the F.B.I." Something in his level look reassured Neil.

"I'm sure that won't be necessary," the doctor said.

For the first time the other man smiled. It broke through the fine lines around his eyes. "We try to take care of our own." Abruptly he turned toward the doors. "You say both doors were locked when you got here?"

Neil thought for a moment. "The front door was. I unlocked it when I came in." His eyes strayed to the kitchen door. He walked to it and turned the knob. It opened easily. Dark color rushed to his face. "What a stupid fool I've been! This door's been unlocked all the time."

"No it hasn't." Parker pointed to the forced window. "If the door had been unlocked when the intruder came, that window wouldn't have been jimmied. Evidently when they left it was through that door."

They stepped outside and into a whirling snowstorm. The storm's intensity had grown ever since Neil got home. "There won't be much sign of footprints. On the other hand, they won't get far in this. I wonder . . ." Parker broke off and stepped to the roadway. "No sign of fresh car tracks since the snow started. They must have left quite a bit earlier in the evening."

Back in the kitchen Neil thought irrelevantly, Margie will have a fit when she sees how we've tracked up her clean floor. The thought vanished as Parker asked, "By any chance, would you know if Miss McCall took her nursing bag with her?"

"I can find out. I know she always has it with her." Neil checked the guest room. "It isn't here."

"Then it appears the girls left of their own will."

The two men stared at each other. This cast a

whole new light on their disappearance.

"But why would Margie go?" Neil asked.

"You told me earlier Misty had been frightened just last night. Margie probably wouldn't let her go off on a call without her."

It made sense. "But what about the jimmied window?"

Parker shook his head. "If I were to reconstruct it, I'd say the girls had gone to bed early. Miss McCall would have been tired after last night's vigil. Evidently their visitor waited until the lights were out, then slipped in the window. I'd guess he counted on making his story about someone sick or hurt strong enough so they wouldn't even be thinking how he got in the house. When a person's mind is strongly on one thing, it isn't until afterward that other details come rushing in."

"And since they had both suddenly come awake when he called them, they wouldn't be their most alert," Neil said.

"That's probably what he counted on. My question is, where could he take them? The other thing — they both distrusted this Van Jones. If he were the man, what kind of concocted story could he give that would be plausible enough for them to fall for it?"

A warning bell rang deep in Neil's mind. "Fall for it." Exactly what he'd asked himself earlier that day. His speech was slow, deliberate. "I just wonder — I was called out today on a false alarm. Someone was supposed to be hurt in a snowmobile accident over toward Dunraven Pass."

"Did they know you went?"

"Of course. They were here when I got the call. A snowmobile was to meet me between here and there. I got there and waited. No one showed. No one had been there, either. On the way home I wondered how he'd gotten word — figured it had probably been a CB radio call. Now I'm not so sure. It could have been a deliberate attempt to get me out of the way."

"If it is, we're dealing with a pretty desperate character."

"I know." Neil swallowed. Then he spoke about Lee Crandall for a few minutes. "I can't help but wonder if this Jones guy is really related to Lee Crandall. The more I compare them, the more they're alike. Maybe he figured I'd never make it back through the storm. Anyone with any knowledge of this area would have seen it coming. If it hadn't been for my trusty jeep, I wouldn't be here now."

"So it could be a personal thing." Parker Wilson shook his head. "I don't like this. I don't like this at all."

Hours earlier, from black depths, someone had called, "Miss McCall! Miss McCall!" The voice came from the hall outside her room.

With a mighty effort Misty roused herself, sat up in bed, shivering. "Who is it?"

"Van Jones. Miss McCall, I hate to bother you,

but there's someone in the log cabin down past mine who needs you. I heard him moaning and went to see if I could help. It's little Mr. Sawyer. He fell coming up the steps and I think his leg's broken. Could you come?"

"What is it?" Margie had awakened.

Misty was already up, calling to the unseen speaker, "Close the door, please. I'll get dressed."

"Who wants you?" Margie asked.

"It's Van Jones. Mr. Sawyer has fallen. I have to go."

"Then I'm going with you."

Misty protested, "It's so cold. Why don't you stay in bed where it's warm?"

"And let you go off with him? Not a chance." Margie had lowered her voice, but already she was nearly dressed. Then she got her parka and boots. "I'm all set." She hesitated for a moment. "Shouldn't we leave a note for Uncle Neil?"

"No. He's probably gone on with the snowmobile outfit to help that man. Besides, even if he comes home while we're gone, he would think we were asleep."

Misty had her nurse's bag. She was checking the contents. Nothing for splints, of course, if the leg really should be broken. On the other hand, there was plenty of wood by all the cabins. Van Jones could get her something to serve temporarily.

"Boy, is it ever snowing!" Margie gasped, clutching her parka hood closer as they stepped out.

For one moment a little stirring inside Misty made her want to run. Were they foolish, going out with this man they distrusted?

Van seemed to catch her reluctance. "It won't take long. See, there's a light in Mr. Sawyer's window. We can cut through the back way." He guided them into a trail in back of the house and office. For one wild second Misty wondered if they could even make it to that lighted window. The storm was really pelting down the snow.

"Right this way." Van skirted a clump of trees, shining a flashlight on the path ahead. His voice was so matter-of-fact, so concerned as he said, "I'd planned to leave today. I didn't get far. It was snowing all around, so I decided I'd better come back until the storm broke." He laughed. "Good thing I did. Poor old Mr. Sawyer probably wouldn't have been able to get help until morning if I hadn't been there. I ran across to your little house first, Miss McCall. When you weren't home I figured you'd be at the doctor's."

Again that faint prickle of alarm. The cold stormy air was clearing Misty's brain in a hurry. "How did you get in?"

"Kitchen door was unlocked." He lied easily. "I knew you were probably tired after being frightened last night, so I stepped in and called."

Margie stopped dead in her tracks. Her voice was low, but accusing. "The kitchen door wasn't unlocked. I locked it myself, just before we went to bed." She grabbed at Misty's arm. "Come on, let's go back and go to Mr. Sawyer's by way of the road."

"Oh, no, you don't!" An ugly revolver had appeared in their trailbreaker's hand. The flashlight in his other hand gleamed on it. "You aren't going anywhere except with me."

Misty was a little dazed. Could this really be happening? "But what about Mr. Sawyer?"

"What about him? He isn't even home. He went to visit some infernal kid somewhere. Just about talked me to death the one time I made the mistake of calling hello." He stepped forward, motioning them with his gun. "Get going. Straight ahead."

"What if we don't? You don't dare shoot us this close to the buildings. Someone would hear," Misty said.

His laugh was as ugly as his revolver. "In this storm? Don't try that on me! I've lived around here enough to know what's going on." He pushed them forward until they bumped into something. A Sno-Cat. What on earth did he have in mind?

"Just why are you doing this? Where are you taking us?"

The authority in Misty's voice forced him to answer. Her blood chilled as he said, "Remember Lee Crandall? He's my big brother."

"Brother! But your name is Jones!"

"Anyone can be named Jones." There was mockery in his voice. "Get in and shut up."

Margie looked at Misty, then back down the

path. Seeing her intention, Misty shook her head slightly. It was too dangerous to risk making a break. She had seen all kinds of patients even in her short career. This man was hovering on the edge of mental illness. He was capable of anything. They would have to go with him if there was to be any chance at all.

It was a ride never to be forgotten. He shoved the girls inside, then took off, driving the Sno-Cat as if he were a maniac. Perhaps he was. So Lee Crandall was his brother. It all fell in place.

Maybe she could get him to talk, Misty thought. "How do you think this is going to help Lee?"

"Why not?" He turned to sneer at her. "The doc and you two sent him where he is. It should make him a whole lot more comfortable to know you three are out of the way!"

Margie huddled closer to Misty, realizing for the first time how slim their chances were. She started to say, "I don't think Lee would want you to do this," but was cut off after the first few words. Van Jones or Crandall or whatever his name was didn't intend to listen to her.

It had turned colder. Even through her heavy parka Misty could feel icy twinges. The speed of the Sno-Cat thrust sharp fingers of freezing air to her face. Jones or Crandall laughed exultantly. He seemed to be enjoying this pitch black night ride. How long they continued Misty never knew. Was it minutes or hours? Their captor seemed to delight in their discomfort.

151

After a time he began to ramble. "Maybe you'd like to hear some stories. Sno-Cat stories." He leered at them.

"These little machines are made for one or two. That's why we're all so cozy." His laughter was enough to drive the girls wild. "They don't have very much power, you know. If we should go into a ravine" — he deliberately headed for one, then at the last minute jerked back — "we wouldn't be able to get out. We could just stay nice and together until the spring thaw. Think you'd like to spend the winter with me in this little baby?" He patted the dash.

Margie had screamed when they headed toward the ravine, but Misty bit her lip. She wouldn't show fear. It might be the only weapon she had. Her laugh was a triumph over fear. "You know, this is really quite exciting!"

Margie looked at her disbelievingly, but Misty warned her with a sharp poke in the ribs. "Van." She leaned closer to him. "I've always secretly wanted to be carried off by a handsome man. If only you'd left Margie behind." She almost gagged at the words. Could anyone, even a lummox like this guy, believe her?

At first he didn't. "What're you trying to give me?"

Again she leaned toward him, whispering in his ear, but loudly enough for Margie to hear. "It's true. I've always gone for the masculine type. Can't we drop Margie off somewhere so we can be alone?"

A convulsive jerk went through his big frame. This chick must really go for him! He could feel an unfamiliar little warmth inside his well-padded body. Outside of Lee, who had ever cared about him? He licked his lips. This nurse was something, really something. What if she would go away with him? He tried to grab the reins of his hatred for her because of Lee. After all, she hadn't really done anything. It had been the other babe.

"We can dump her right here."

This was the one thing Misty had feared, the chance she had to take. Now she deliberately made her voice light. "Oh, that would never do. They'll have helicopters out in the morning looking for anything that moves. Besides, we wouldn't want to spoil our honeymoon by re-membering we'd killed someone."

"Honeymoon!" The Sno-Cat jumped forward.

Misty's fingers on Margie's wrist dug in, a mute warning not to say one word. They wouldn't have been needed. If her life depended on it, and perhaps it did, Margie couldn't have forced out a sound.

"Why, of course. I'm not the type of girl who would run off with a man who wouldn't marry me."

The words hung in the frosty air between them. Had she gone too far? Had she made the bait so obvious he wouldn't swallow it? But she was dealing with an unstable mentality. It could go either way.

Van Jones didn't answer immediately. So this doll wanted him to marry her. Well, why not? A cruel smile crossed his face. Promise her anything. It wouldn't matter — in the long run. He hadn't bargained for this when he kidnapped the girls. He'd been going to leave them somewhere out in the open, too far away from anywhere to get back. By the time they could be rescued, he'd be long gone.

He looked at the sky. The snow had stopped. There were millions of stars. Tomorrow would be clear. That hadn't been part of his plan. He had banked on at least one more day of bad weather. Misty was right. Tomorrow they'd be out with choppers, planes, everything. Whatever he did, it would have to be tonight.

Was she faking it, pretending to care? What difference did it make? He'd have a mighty pretty hostage if worse came to worst.

"All right, baby, if that's how you want it." He swung in a wide arc, heading in a little different direction.

"Wh-where are you taking me?" Margie had found her voice.

"Norris Junction."

Norris Junction! Why that was only about twenty miles from Mammoth! Misty pressed Margie's arm so she wouldn't cry out. But it wasn't so easy as they had thought. The time they had been in the Sno-Cat they had not been heading toward Norris Junction. It was after four o'clock in the morning when their wild night ride was over, at least for Margie.

The Sno-Cat slowed, stopped. "This is as far as you go." When Margie didn't move, Van barked, "Get out before I throw you out!"

Slowly, her legs buckling from the long hours of inactivity, she climbed awkwardly to the ground.

"But, Van, I thought we were taking her to Norris Junction."

"Close enough." He pointed across what seemed an endless white expanse. "Right that way, ma'am. About five miles. Just keep walking. You'll get there."

Misty's heart sank. Five miles across that snowy road? She could sense they had come to a road, but with all the snow, every step would be torture for Margie. If she slowed down too much there was always danger of freezing to death.

"Margie." Her voice was sharp. "No matter how tired you get, keep on walking. Do you understand? *Keep on walking.* The chill factor out here is terrible. Don't stop to rest. No matter how slowly, just keep on walking."

She caught Van's black look and added in a lighter tone, "After all, you're the one who has to tell everyone I've eloped with Van."

If only she could send a more personal message to Neil! He would understand she had done what she had to do in order to save Margie, but he would never know how much she had cared. She knew beyond a certainty there would be no way back for her. Van Jones or Crandall would never marry her. He wouldn't risk it. He'd keep her somewhere until she either escaped, or he no longer felt safe. Then he'd kill her.

Before I ever let him touch me, I'll force this Sno-Cat over a cliff. The promise to herself reassured her, gave her strength to meet Margie's eyes squarely in the starlight. "Tell Dr. Rogers I won't be able to accept his proposition on account of a sudden engagement." It was the only thing she could think of that would let him know there had never been a fiancé in her life. She knew from the way he had treated her lately Margie had passed on her choice bit of news. In that moment the picture of the girl in Neil's wallet didn't intrude. It was important he know she had cared, even though it would be too late.

"Good-bye, Margie, I'll send you a postcard." Play it out to the end. Force a smile. Wave gaily. Then, "What are we waiting for, Van?"

They disappeared gradually from Margie's sight, becoming only a moving dot in the starlight, then nothing at all.

Margie watched them out of sight, struggling to keep back tears. If only she could have been the one to go away with Van. It was all her fault, anyway, getting tangled up with that Lee Crandall. Now Misty was sacrificing herself to save her.

"What can I do?" Her cry of anguish startled an owl nearby. With a "whoo-whoo" he was up and gone, seeking refuge in another tree away from this human figure so alone in the night.

For one awful moment Margie felt as if she could just sink down in place and die. Maybe it would be better for everyone. She'd brought tragedy and unhappiness to her family, to Uncle Neil, and now to Misty. But something of her uncle's spirit lay deep inside Margie, untouched until now. After that one outburst she lifted her chin.

"I can't die here. If I do, no one will know where Misty is. I've got to get to Norris Junction."

It was the determination of a girl suddenly faced with life and death responsibilities. The housework had toughened her a bit, but the knowledge of Misty's life hanging in the balance gave Margie the strength to accomplish what she did.

Step after step. Sinking through the snow. Snow in her boots, stopping, dumping it out. The time came when she had no feeling in either feet or hands. She had no way of knowing what time it was; her watch lay on her dresser at home.

Once she knew she'd never make it. She had to stop and rest. But from within her mind came Misty's words: *Keep on walking*. She did. One foot after the other. No feeling. No life.

When she got to the place where she couldn't go on, she whipped herself with the memory of Misty's face as she said, "Tell Dr. Rogers . . . sudden engagement . . ." Everything was all mixed up. *Keep on walking*.

At her lowest ebb another thought came, one

that would provide the last necessary ounce of stamina to get her through. Jim Robinson. What would he say? She had to tell him. She was sorry. Never should have got mixed up with Lee Crandall. Would Jim care?

"I can't go to the Ice Carnival. I can't go to the Ice Carnival." She had to tell Jim. She had to tell Uncle Neil something. What was it?

Something solid loomed before her. Was it a mirage? Could people see mirages in the snow? She had thought they were only on the desert. She reached out. Nothing there. With a little cry she collapsed. There was light, then oblivion.

Why did her feet and hands ache so? Why did she feel so cold? Was that her own voice babbling, "I have to tell Uncle Neil. Where is he? Misty, don't go! He won't marry you!"

If only she could open her eyes, get away from this terrible nightmare! Was that Neil calling? She tried to answer, but there was no way she could get through the darkness. Something warm and wet was sliding down her throat. She shivered again. Was this what it was like to be dead?

"She's slipped into a coma." They were the last words she heard.

But Neil Rogers and Parker Wilson, standing above her bed, looked at each other in despair. The girl lying spent and quiet was the only key to what had happened. From her broken sentences they had managed to piece together a little of what had happened. Had Misty gone away with her captor to save Margie? Until the desperately ill girl came around and could tell them, there was no way to know. The helicopters were out, searching. Yet how did they even know which way to look until Margie regained consciousness? In the meantime, where was Misty? More important, what was happening to her?

Chapter 11

When Van swung the Sno-Cat away, leaving Margie standing in the snow, Misty was at her lowest ebb. She was going to die. Either he would kill her, or she would run them over a ravine edge. She would never allow herself to be alone with him any place other than the Sno-Cat. When he reached over to leer at her and pat her shoulder, it took every ounce of courage she had not to scream. Not yet. They were still close enough for him to go back after Margie. That mustn't happen.

"Honeymoon, huh, baby! Think you'll like a honeymoon in this cold place?" His laugh was crude, chilling. "When we get to the cabin I'll keep you warm."

"Cabin?" The word burst from her throat.

"You bet. You don't think I'm going to take a chance on getting spotted come daylight, do you?"

"But what about getting married?" Anything to stall him.

His eyes narrowed into slits. "It will have to wait. Can't chance it yet."

There went her last line of defense. She had hoped to at least get him delayed for a while. She was getting colder and colder. She couldn't mention it — he'd probably grab her. If he did it would mean the end for both of them. They had left the more open areas and were traveling along a ridged expanse. One move out of him and she'd see they went over that ridge. Better that than be at his mercy in some lonely cabin.

"You know, baby, you're going to get to like me real well. I know you were putting me on about wanting to get kidnapped and all that but you'll learn to like me — a whole lot."

Misty shuddered inside but kept her voice even. "I'll like you a whole lot more after we get married."

In the pale dimness just before dawn she could see his faint grin. "Sure you will."

Day was breaking when he swung back into a particular clump of trees. The snow was deep and the trees dense. Misty's heart sank. Searching helicopters and planes would never find them in that place. The Sno-Cat would be as hidden from sight as the log cabin slowly emerging from the forest. This, then, would be her last stand. She almost giggled nervously. Just call her Melissa Custer! How could she think of such a thing now?

"Welcome home, baby!" He stopped in front of the cabin. It was a far cry from her own log cabin. There were staring holes for windows, un-hampered by glass. The door had long since rotted and fallen from its hinges. The entire place was dark. Cobwebs hung in the open doorway. She couldn't go in there, she just couldn't! But what else could she do?

Before she knew his intention Van snatched her from the Sno-Cat, carried her into the cabin, and set her on her feet. The look in his eyes was madder than ever. What had she done? Should she have just let him ditch them both out in the middle of nowhere? At least Margie was spared this, she told herself. A vision of Margie as she had last seen her, standing in the middle of that terribly white-blanketed area, rose to haunt her. Maybe Margie wouldn't make it, either. Then her sacrifice would be for nothing.

"I'll get a fire started. Just a little one. I don't want smoke giving away where we are, although no one will be looking for us here. You can see the trade at this inn is pretty slim." His smile was cruel, degrading. "After we get the fire started, we'll have the whole day to be here together. Tonight we'll make a run for it." He grinned back from the doorway. "Too bad it isn't the Hilton, but it will do for now." He was gone, leaving Misty in the middle of the cabin.

For one moment she just stood there, watching him leave. He was across the little clearing, into the edge of the timber. If she were to jump in the Sno-Cat and take off, could she get away before he recrossed the clearing? He had probably counted on her being too dumb to even get the Sno-Cat started if she wanted to. Or maybe he was convinced of his own charm enough to think she wanted to be here! Well, that had been her intention, hadn't it?

Crawling on all fours so he couldn't see her,

Misty crept to the Sno-Cat, thanking God she had watched how he had manipulated the levers. It was well she did.

Just before he started tearing dead limbs from a low-growing tree, he looked back. This might prove to be an interesting day! She was older than he, but pretty. Small and pretty. He daydreamed a bit. Maybe he would just keep her. It would be nice to have one like her around.

His daydream was interrupted by a loud noise. Misty had managed to start the Sno-Cat. "Stop that machine!" In an instant he was running toward her.

She frantically pushed and pulled levers. One caught. A surge of hope mingled with tears on her cheeks as she leaped forward — but not quite soon enough. The next moment he had flung himself at her, furiously trying to wrest the controls from her inexperienced hands. She wouldn't let him. She would never go back in that cabin with him.

From deep inside came a cry for help. In a split second she remembered the faith of her mother. "When there's no way out, there's always a way up." Now she voiced that faith. "God, help me!"

The man who was tearing at her fingers cursed. With a mighty wrench he got the controls — but too late! They were on the edge of the ravine crest, back in the open. One moment they were on safe ground, the next they were falling . . . falling. . . .

Parker Wilson had kept lines crackling all morning. There were helicopters out searching, observing every inch of space visible from the air, ever widening their circles.

"I only hope he doesn't have sense enough to get into the trees," he told Dr. Rogers. "I'm afraid he will, though. Evidently he knows this area well."

Dr. Rogers had dark smudges of weariness on his face. "I'd give everything I own to be out there searching with them!"

"You're needed right here." Parker nodded to the motionless form on the cot.

Margie still lay in a coma. There was no telling when she would come out of it — if ever. Yet Dr. Rogers had to be there when she did.

"We're doing everything we can," Parker added.

Neil was still thinking of Parker's words at noon. The sky was cobalt blue. Only a few clouds marred its blue expanse. It was a perfect day for a search. He shuddered.

"Dr. Rogers!" Parker Wilson was breathing heavily. "I just got word." He paused for breath. The look on his face was serious.

Neil felt as if his heart had stopped. "What is it?"

"The choppers have spotted the Sno-Cat." Sympathy wrinkled Parker's forehead. "I hate to tell you, but it's upside down in a ravine. The ironic thing is, it isn't too far from Mammoth. There's an old rundown cabin. Van Crandall or

Jones or whoever he is must have known about it and was heading for there."

Neil's face was ghastly. "How long will it take to get a rescue party out there?"

"They're already on their way." Wilson looked at the quiet form. "Could she be moved?"

"Why?"

"We can land a chopper here. I know she'd be a whole lot better off back in your clinic at Mammoth."

"Let's get going. We can move her, but we'll do it carefully."

"Don't worry about that. This particular chopper pilot can take off and land as if you were sitting in a rocking chair."

He was right. Within a short time Margie had been transported to Mammoth. Now if only Misty could be found safe! Neil had to face it. Upside down in a Sno-Cat in the bottom of a ravine didn't sound promising. Yet, wouldn't she be better off dead than in the hands of a man like Van Crandall?

If only I had told her I loved her. If only I hadn't alienated her. The dull thoughts beat through Neil's brain. *I can't even be in the rescue party. At least, she'll have good care. Parker said Ginger had come down from Gardiner, and her boss with her. They're both in the rescue party. He's a good doctor. He'll be able to do whatever's necessary, if anything.*

During the following hours Neil felt himself become an old man. All he could do was wait. He was helpless, tied to his vigil with Margie. Once she seemed to rouse, whispering something, but she lapsed into unconsciousness again.

When Parker Wilson stepped back into Neil's office, his face was grim.

"What did you find?" Neil was on his feet, face white.

"The Sno-Cat. Crandall or Jones. Dead."

"And Misty?"

Parker's eyes noted the total absence of color in the doctor's face. How he loved the girl! "Footprints leading away from the Sno-Cat."

"Then she's alive! Thank God!"

The hardest thing Parker Wilson had ever done was to shake his head. "We don't know that." He spoke gruffly. "She was alive when she made those footprints. But now? We don't know. That Sno-Cat accident must have occurred shortly after daybreak. The man had been dead several hours. That means Misty has been wandering all that time.

"If she keeps on going she's fine. If she stops to rest, or has some weakening injury . . ." He left it unsaid, but Neil knew what it meant.

"I'm going after her."

"What about Margie?"

"She's still unconscious, although she has shown signs of coming to. Besides, you brought Ginger's boss back with you, didn't you? I'm sure Dr. Smith won't mind watching Margie."

"You're right, Dr. Rogers." A balding man in a heavy coat had walked in. He was competent-looking, brisk. "I'd be no good on following a trail in the snow. Too much weight. But I can stay here."

"I'm going back again with you." Ginger had also come in. She saw the looks of protest on their faces. "Save your breath. Nothing can keep me from going back. Besides" — she turned and whistled — "Reddy here can help us find Misty."

"Reddy! How did you get him?" Neil stared at the red setter already leaping toward him, wagging his tail in delight.

"Don't you remember I took him home with me? He may be the hospital pet in summer, but he has to have a home in winter. The doctor who used to keep him has moved. He's my dog now. When we found the Sno-Cat wreck, he wanted to follow that trail right then and there, but we came back for heavier clothing and something to eat. She has a big start on us."

Ginger's freckles stood out on her creamy skin. Strange, Dr. Rogers had never noticed them before. Now the agony in her eyes for her friend matched that in Neil's own.

"All right, Ginger. You're trained for it."

"We have to find her before dark." Parker Wilson had assumed command of the new rescue party. There were five of them. Neil, Ginger, Parker, and two rangers who would carry the stretcher.

It didn't take long to get to the scene of the Sno-Cat. It lay, a grotesque reminder of their grim errand, at the bottom of the ravine.

"The only thing I can think happened is she

must have some way gotten control of the Sno-Cat. The man must have been underneath when they landed. Otherwise she'd have been killed instantly."

"Then he did in death what he had never done in life — saved someone else." Ginger wished she had held back the words. Yet it was true.

"He's probably better off. There's a stiff penalty for kidnapping," Neil said.

"Attempted murder, too. He could never have let her go. She would have been a witness against him," Parker joined in.

Ginger cried out, "I still don't understand why she would go off with him!"

"The only thing we can figure out from Margie's babbling is Misty must have somehow convinced the guy she liked him. Margie kept saying, 'He won't marry you, Misty.' But until she comes back to consciousness, we won't know that, either."

Neil's throat was tight. "I think she was trying to save Margie."

It ended the conversation right then and there. Besides, they were busy following Reddy. He had faithfully followed the tracks in the snow.

"You know, that dog's really amazing! He isn't trained for bloodhound work, yet he's kept to the trail."

"It's because he loves Misty. After all, she took a stone from his paw her very first night in Yellowstone."

Ginger's words brought back a flood of memories to Neil. How well he remembered his own first meetings with Misty! To think he had ever thought her a boy! He grinned wryly. She was as unlike a boy as anyone he had ever known! Now, if only they could find her alive.

Was it minutes or hours until they heard Reddy's joyful bark? He had raced ahead. Neil felt his breath catch and began to run. Would it really be Misty? Or had Reddy been sidetracked by something else?

It was Misty. Pale as death she lay sprawled in the snow. She must have gone until she was worn out. Neil spotted a root sticking up through the snow. Evidently she had caught her foot and fallen. Instantly he was beside her. He felt color come back into his face. She was alive. Suffering from exposure, scratched from what must have been many falls, she was still alive.

There was a look in his face so filled with reverence the others turned away. Ginger told Misty weeks later it had been like glimpsing the holy of holies. If ever she had wondered whether Neil Rogers cared, that look told her more than she had dared guess.

It wasn't an easy trip back. Misty was a dead weight on the stretcher. The four men took turns carrying it.

Once Ginger laughed, more like a sob, and commented, "Good thing she's so small and light. If it were me, we'd never make it!"

No one even noticed the incongruity of her statement. They were too anxious to get back to

Mammoth, warmth, and medical facilities to help Misty.

At last they made it. They staggered into Neil's home with their burden.

"Take her upstairs. We'll put her to bed in the guest room." Instantly he became all doctor, crisp and professional. "Ginger, get her undressed. Get her into those flannel pajamas I saw up there, and her robe. Pile covers on her. She's so tired I'd rather not try and put her in a warm tub. We'll do that later if she doesn't respond." He turned to Parker. "Can you cook?"

"You bet. I'll heat some broth."

"Coffee, too."

"She hates coffee," Ginger put in.

"I know. But it will bring her around." He had already pulled off Misty's gloves and chafed her hands until they were warm.

By the time Ginger had her undressed and in bed, the coffee and broth were ready. It was the warm liquid going down her throat that reached the depths for Misty. The broth slid down easily, but when it came to the coffee she rebelled, even in her semi-conscious state. She choked and fought it.

"Give her more broth." The coffee was taken away.

Hours later Misty came out of her sleep to a state of being half awake. Was she seeing a rerun? Dr. Rogers was asleep in a chair by her bed in crumpled clothing. Had he been there all night? Or was it still night? She moved restlessly, trying to remember. Where had she been? Why was he in her room? But this wasn't her room!

Everything began to swim again. She wasn't in her log cabin. She was in the guest room at Neil's home. In spite of her confusion, she remembered how she'd felt when she first went to that room with Margie. Was it last night? It had been like coming home.

She lapsed back into a half sleep but roused as Neil came to the bed. Her tongue felt thick. She was too tired to explain. His words from so long ago kept whirling in her mind: ". . . Marry me, marry me . . ." She'd been so much trouble to him. Keeping him up watching over her, even though she couldn't remember why.

Finally her words came out. "It might be better if I marry you."

From somewhere she could hear a sound of movement. Then warm lips pressed her own. "I think you'd better," he said.

"Home." Misty was asleep, leaving Neil Rogers standing above her, staring down at her still form. His heart beat fast. Had she meant it? A dreadful thought came to him. Maybe she hadn't even known who he was! Maybe in her confusion she thought he was that man she had promised to marry. Yet hadn't her lips responded to his kiss?

I'll never let her go. The determined set to his jaw startled Ginger, who had come in.

"I'll relieve you. Go get some sleep."

He looked at her, then back at the girl who was

171

sun, moon, and stars to his world. Without a word he stepped out. But it was not to sleep. He went straight to his room, moved aside a picture, and opened a small wall safe. From it he withdrew a velvet jewel case. There were various pieces in it, a few brooches, one necklace. They were all pushed aside. He held up a ring, so tiny it appeared lost in his big hand. The setting was old-fashioned, but the diamond was beautiful. In the lamplight it sparkled, its facets gleaming. It was not large or gaudy, but one of the finest diamonds of its kind.

Tomorrow he would offer it to her. It had been his own mother's whose hand was as slim as Misty's.

Again he looked at the ring, thinking of his mother as she had told him, "Someday you will meet a woman you want to spend your whole life with, loving, having children, in joy and sorrow. If she will accept my ring, I will be proud to know she has also accepted my son." His mother's hands were no longer slim when she had given it to him. She had put aside the ring.

Tomorrow. A daring gleam came into the tired eyes, lighting them, in spite of the fact Dr. Rogers had had no sleep for two nights. He picked up the ring. Would it fit?

"I'll do it!"

Reddy, who had fallen asleep on the rug by his bed, looked up in surprise. A boyish grin went over Neil's face. "That's what I'll do right now.

172

Then there will be no chance of any misunderstandings!"

Ginger looked up in surprise as he appeared in the doorway. "I thought you'd gone to sleep."

She was amazed to see the glint in his eyes as he whispered, "I have a claim to stake first." To her amazement, he deliberately walked to the bed, picked up Misty's inert left hand, and slipped a ring on her engagement finger!

Ginger gasped, looking at him, but he had regained his usual cool manner. "See that she sleeps well, Miss Snapp."

The door softly closed behind him leaving Ginger alone with Misty, her own amazement, and a diamond ring shooting sparks from the dim nightlight by Misty's bed.

Chapter 12

Something hard and sharp was pressing into Misty's cheek. She opened her eyes and turned her head away. Suddenly the events of the previous day rushed through her. Was it a rock leaving a deep imprint on her face? She moved her left hand, trying to dislodge the rock. But it was not the snowy outlines of forests and ravines she saw. This was the familiar wallpaper in the guest room at Neil Rogers's home. Then what could be hurting her?

"Good grief!"

Her short exclamation brought Ginger on the run. Misty was sitting up in bed staring at the diamond ring. The storm outside had vanished. Brilliant sunlight streamed through the window, but its sparks were no brighter than those of the diamond on her engagement finger. "Where did this come from?"

Ginger almost choked to hide her excitement. She had spent most of the night trying to figure it out. Now she only said, "Dr. Rogers put it on last night. He said he was staking his claim."

Misty could only stare at her, more bewildered than ever. "Staking his claim! That means taking possession, doesn't it?"

"Yes it does." Ginger's curiosity overcame her hesitancy. "Did you tell him you'd marry him?"

Misty was silent for a long moment. "I might have."

"Might have!" This time it was Ginger's turn to stare. "You mean you don't know whether you promised to marry him or not?"

"That's about it." Misty looked perplexed, trying to remember. "I was so half asleep. Someone came in. I remember saying something about it might be better if I married him."

Ginger was on tiptoe with amazement. "Then *you* proposed to *him?*"

Misty flushed. "I hope not."

"What did he answer?"

"I'm not sure. I think he said I should."

"Of all the proposals! Misty McCall, you really beat everything. You actually dare lie there and tell me that on the strength of that he came back in and put that engagement ring on your finger?"

"I guess he must have. It's there." She faltered. "Do you think he just put it there because — because he feels sorry for me?"

"Sorry for you! You are naive. Misty, Neil Rogers has been mad about you since long before we left Lake."

A voice from the doorway broke in. "What observant big eyes you have, Grandmother Snapp. Now if you'll excuse us, I'd like to talk to my fiancée alone."

Whew! That was dismissal if she'd ever heard one! But Ginger wasn't even daunted. "Certainly, Dr. Rogers. When you're through with your patient, I'll be back to help her change."

"Good-bye, Miss Snapp." There wasn't a trace of emotion in Neil's cool voice, nothing to show he had both dreaded and longed for the coming interview.

"Well, you certainly got rid of Ginger in one big hurry." Misty was eyeing him a little dubiously. She couldn't seem to control her bouncing heart. When he turned toward the bed, she clenched her right hand over her left.

"Don't try to hide your engagement ring, my dear. By the way, do you mind the old-fashioned setting or should I take it off and have it reset for you?"

The same demon of perversity that had caused Misty to tell Margie she planned to be married took possession of her again. He was so tall, so sure of himself standing there. Ginger had said he loved her, but there was nothing in his attitude to show it. He almost acted as if he had made a good business deal. Wanting to strike out, to rouse him out of his coolness, she answered, "I want you to take it off and leave it off." He only smiled. It infuriated her even more. "Have you so soon forgotten the man I plan to marry?"

"Of course not. But you'll have to. After all, last night when you asked me to marry you —"

"I asked you to marry me?" Misty's gasp was lost as he completed his sentence as if she had never interrupted.

"And I accepted; it was with the understanding you'd do the decent thing and tell the other man you now had other commitments."

Misty was speechless. The audacity of him! She asked him to marry her? He had accepted? Tears of anger sparkled on lashes.

"Don't feel bad, Misty. After all, this is Leap Year. It was perfectly proper for you to ask for what you wanted. Besides, as I told you once before, in order to live here in my house after Margie is gone, you'll have to marry me. I can't have my reputation tarnished." He bent over, kissed her lightly on the cheek, and went out.

Misty felt torn apart. All the hope she had had when Ginger said Neil loved her was dead. All he wanted was a housekeeper when Margie left, someone to see his home was taken care of, just a convenience. She looked at the ring. Something in its very old-fashionedness seemed to quiet her. All right. If that's what he wanted, that's what he'd get. She'd marry him, all right. But he'd find she was someone to reckon with once they were married! What better place to win his love than right here in his home as his wife?

Misty's decision made her face flush, but it also settled her down. Mischief filled the blue eyes. She had to lower the lids in order to hide it from Ginger.

"Everything settled?"

"Yes. We're getting married."

Ginger looked at her suspiciously. There was something missing in her friend's voice. There should have been breathlessness, more excitement. "Are you sure you want to marry him, Misty?"

"Quite sure." Even irrepressible Ginger couldn't go beyond the reserve in Misty's tone. She said no more but went about getting Misty washed and ready for the day.

"No, you can't get up. Dr. Rogers says you are to spend at least one day in bed. Later this afternoon Parker Wilson will want to talk with you, get a full report of what happened during your kidnapping."

A shadow filled Misty's eyes. "Ginger! I haven't even asked about Margie."

"She's getting better. She's been a pretty sick girl, but this morning she opened her eyes. She's been lapsing in and out of consciousness."

"I'm getting up. I have to see her." Misty threw back the covers, but Ginger forced her back on the pillows. "Not until Dr. Rogers says so." She stepped to the doorway and called, "Dr. Rogers, will you come in, please?"

The man who entered the room was not the confident fiancé. He was the professional man Misty had learned to admire. "Patient giving you some trouble?"

"Not really. She just wants to see Margie."

Neil's eyes softened as he saw the pleading look in Misty's face. It couldn't hurt her. Fortunately, she had escaped without injury. "Just put on a warm robe and slippers. I think it might help Margie. She seems to be groping for reality. She keeps mumbling something about 'sudden engagement' and 'can't go to Ice Festival.' If she hears your voice, Misty, perhaps it will give her something to hang on to when the next wave comes."

Margie looked small and white in the bed. Her hands plucked nervously at the covers. But when Misty took her hand and said clearly, "It's all right, Margie, I'm here and *everything is all right*," she seemed to relax. A moment later she was breathing deeply.

"She's fallen into a natural sleep. It's the thing she needs most." Neil gently led Misty from the room. She saw the look in his eyes but steeled herself against it. Probably just gratitude for what she'd done for Margie. Yet inside a little voice whispered, Perhaps your job of making him love you won't be so hard after all.

Margie slept all that day, then the next. It had been decided to wait until she was better for Parker Wilson to get the whole story.

"No use for Miss McCall to have to relive it twice," Neil had decreed.

It was a full week later when Margie, in robe and slippers, Misty, who had recovered miraculously, Ginger, Neil, Parker Wilson, and — of all people — Frank Jensen and Jim Robinson gathered around the big fireplace.

Frank and Jim had been in touch with Ginger and as soon as Margie was out of danger they had surprised the little household at Mammoth by coming down from college.

"Now, Miss McCall. Miss Crawford," Parker

179

said kindly, "please tell us everything that happened, from the time you awakened until you got back here to Mammoth."

The story was pitifully short to cover all the events that had occurred. When Margie came to the part where Misty played up to Van, her voice broke. "I knew she shouldn't do it, but she dug her elbow in my ribs for me to keep silent. I began to think that since she was a nurse maybe she could handle him." She shuddered and Jim Robinson clenched his teeth.

"I walked and walked. I didn't think I could make it. I was so cold. But Misty had said no matter how tired I got, to keep on walking. I thought of her out there all alone. She had given me a message for Uncle Neil. I *had* to make it. Finally, I bumped into something. I remember falling. That's all." She closed her eyes. "I can't remember what I was supposed to tell you, Uncle Neil."

"Don't worry about it. Misty can tell me herself — after we're married."

"Married!" Margie's eyes popped open. "You're getting married?"

"I can't lose the best nurse I ever had to kidnappers. From now on she'll be right where I can keep an eye on her."

"But what about that other man, the one you planned to marry?" Margie's eyes were accusing, but deep inside she knew, from Misty's look, there had never been any other man.

"We'll talk about it later." Dr. Rogers still held

180

center stage. "Right now we want to hear what happened to Misty after they left in the Sno-Cat. We've managed to piece things together, but would like the entire story."

Misty's hands were clenched in her lap, her eyes downcast as she finished the story. "I thought we'd never get anywhere. Then we came to that horrible cabin." She shuddered, thinking of it. "He grabbed me from the Sno-Cat, shoved me inside, and said we'd spend the day. We'd travel that night when no one could see us."

Revulsion washed through her. "I made up my mind death would be better than staying there with him. I really think he'd crossed the border from sanity to insanity. Anyway, he went to get wood for a fire. He must not have thought I'd know anything about a Sno-Cat. I didn't. But I was desperate.

"I managed to get it started, but not in time. He jumped me, fought for the controls. Suddenly we were falling into nowhere. When I awakened, I was upside down in the Sno-Cat. But he was underneath me. Very still. I checked his pulse and heartbeat. There were none. Yet my life had been saved. I remember saying a prayer just before we went over. I guess God must have heard and answered."

There was a long silence before she continued. "I knew I'd freeze if I stayed there. I felt sick, dizzy, but I had to get moving. I don't know how far I walked. It seemed like miles. Then I tripped. I was too tired to get up, too tired to care."

Only the crackle of the fire broke the stillness. Each of those present was busy with differing thoughts. Margie and Misty were reliving the horror of that wild night ride and its aftermath. Dr. Rogers's jaw was set, thinking of what could have happened. Ginger felt cold and reached out to Frank for reassurance. His warm hand closed over her own. Parker Wilson switched off the tape recorder on which he had captured the testimony.

It was for Jim Robinson to voice their thoughts. "I'm glad it's over." He bent an unreadable look on Margie, then added, "By the way, you'll all be hale and hearty for the Ice Carnival in a few weeks, won't you?"

Neil snatched up the comment. Let the past be gone. Both of the girls looked tired. "You bet." He plunged rashly ahead. "In fact, Misty and I are planning to get married during the Ice Carnival. Right, Misty?"

If her face showed how stunned she felt, Misty hid it well. "Right, Neil."

But before anyone could comment Margie asked, "Then if you'll be here to take care of Uncle Neil and everything — would it be all right, I mean, do you think I could get enrolled in a nursing course?"

Blank amazement greeted her question.

"It will be right at the beginning of second semester and everything. I just thought it might be a good time." She hesitated, then her chin went up. It was significant how she looked at each one in turn, but let her eyes rest on Jim Robinson as she made her confession. "I've been pretty use-less for a long time. It's only since I started keeping house for Uncle Neil that I've really learned a lot. I'd like to take a practical nursing course. I don't feel I have the ability to become an R.N. but practical nurses are needed, too."

Neil recovered first. "They sure are." He walked across and kissed Margie soundly. "Who knows? By the time you finish your course, Misty may want to quit nursing for a while and have a baby." He ignored her outraged gasp. Really, he was going too far! "You could come back and help me, Margie."

Jim Robinson had a word. "Or she might be getting married about then." There was direct challenge in his statement.

Margie turned red and laughed. "Maybe I will. Time will tell."

When they had all gone, Neil turned to Misty. He had asked her to wait. He had something to discuss. For a moment he dreaded turning to-ward her, but there was no sign of it in his face as he said, "Well, Miss McCall, seems you have a double job coming up." If he had expected fire-works he was doomed to disappointment.

She only smiled calmly. "Seems I have." And she walked out of the room, head held high, every ounce of her showing dignity.

Was that a muffled chuckle from the good doctor? Misty didn't know and wouldn't wait to find out. So he thought he could just dispose of her by saying, "Come here, go there." He was in for one big surprise. When she was Mrs. Doctor Neil Rogers he was in for the shock of his life. She'd see to that! She might be small, but she could fight, and that's what she'd do. He might think he'd marry her, get a housekeeper, even a wife. What he didn't know was just how much of a wife he was getting! She'd show him his mighty-male tactics didn't go over with her. In the meantime she'd better get ready for a wedding — her own.

Chapter 13

There were ice sculptures everywhere! Never had Misty or Margie seen such beauty. The weather had cooperated perfectly with the college Ice Carnival. First had come the snow to make the sculptures; then had come blazing winter days and icy nights, to keep them in a state of perfection.

"I can't believe the variety!" Margie's eyes were round. "Look at that one!"

Misty looked and laughed. A full-scale sculpture of Santa Claus stuck in a chimney had been given realism by actual smoke coming from his pipe! Yet it was only one of the creations. Cartoon characters, entire miniature villages, famous people — the list was endless.

Looking at Margie it was hard to believe she was the same beaten girl who had faltered to safety just a few weeks before. Christmas had come and gone quietly for them. There had been the celebration for park employees still at Mammoth, but they had not been part of it. It was too close to the near tragedy. But now, with the second semester just starting, the girls were free. Or were they? Margie had never been happier. She was all enrolled for her LPN course. Ginger and Frank were preparing for their summer wedding.

Only Misty alternated between joy and despair. Sometimes she would catch a look on Neil Rogers's face that sent her spirits soaring. Other times, helping him in the clinic, she was a necessary machine. Which was he marrying?

Day after day she wondered. If only something would happen to assure her he loved her the way she did him! But what? There was no Van Crandall around to kidnap her again — thank God! She still had nightmares when she thought of it. What could she do? Come right out and ask him?

She had even rehearsed a little speech in her own room. "I have to know if you really love me or just need a housekeeper plus." Even to her own ears it sounded ridiculous. Could she stage some kind of scene for his benefit, anything to shake him out of his iron control?

He always kissed her good morning and good night. But not the way he had kissed her so furiously at Lake. Not the way he had kissed her the night he slipped the ring on her finger. She had come to remember that night, how she'd told him maybe she should marry him and the kiss that followed. Now his kisses were cool, controlled, almost clinical!

Misty shivered, not from the outdoor chill, but from her own thoughts. Could she go through with her original plan to marry Neil and hope to make him really fall in love with her afterward? At times she thought she could not. Other times it seemed the only way. If she didn't marry him, her pride wouldn't allow her to stay in Mammoth. She would have to go away, never see him again. *I couldn't stand that.*

She stared at one ice sculpture until Margie called, "Come on, Misty, there's lots more to see!"

Margie was in wonderful spirits. Perhaps the Christmas present from Jim Robinson had done it. A tiny heart on a fine chain. Only Margie had seen the even tinier message tucked in the box — "I give you a heart."

She had hurriedly slipped it in her pocket, showing only the necklace. She wore it everywhere, even to bed at night. It had become a symbol of Someday.

Although Ginger was caught up in the joy of being with Frank, enjoying the Ice Carnival, her keen eyes were troubled. All was not right with Misty. She knew her too well to be fooled by the bright pretense her friend was making. What could be wrong?

Misty loved Neil Rogers, and Neil worshipped her. But there was something amiss. Neil couldn't be at the festival. But that wasn't it. Try as she would, Ginger had been unable to put her finger on exactly what it was. She had approached Misty in several ways, hoping to understand. Each time she met with that invisible wall that had been raised between them. She could not penetrate it without coming right out and asking. She could not do that.

So while Misty laughed and watched the Ice

Carnival, wondering about Neil, Ginger laughed and watched Misty. As the hours passed Misty became more brittle until Ginger thought she would crack. Her laughter grew higher, as if to assure everyone what a wonderful time she was having. She eagerly pointed out the sights. No one suspected she was putting on an act — except Ginger.

It had been arranged for Neil and Misty to be married in the little stone chapel at Mammoth. Misty had been adamant about it. "I don't want to be married in the middle of an Ice Carnival. I want a small wedding, with just our group there, and I want it in the stone chapel."

Her wishes held. They would be married the week after the Ice Festival. Jim and Margie, and Frank and Ginger would come. So would the former Mammoth doctor and his good wife, and Nora Maloney, who lived in Gardiner. That would be all, except for the minister.

Misty's dress hung in her little log cabin bedroom, a drift of white. Simple in style, it set off beautifully her blue eyes and long hair.

"Don't get some outlandish hairstyle for your wedding," Ginger advised. "Wear it as you always do. I've seen too many brides whose wedding pictures didn't even look like them because of some hairdresser."

Misty would spend the week between the Ice Carnival and her wedding back in her own log cabin. In some ways she welcomed it. It would give her time to think, to discover if she really wanted to go through with it. If she didn't, she'd just disappear. She never gave a thought as to how it could be accomplished. With the snow and everything, any way she would go was certain to be known to Neil.

While Misty and Ginger were stewing and fretting, Neil Rogers was literally holding his breath. His giant bluff seemed to be working, far more than he had dreamed! He hadn't really thought Misty would accept the situation. Just the thread of her whispered, "It might be better if I'd marry you" was fragile, not enough to really consider as a firm "yes" to a proposal. Sometimes he paced his room at night thinking about it. Should he tell Misty that was all it had been, just a half-coherent comment?

No! He could make her love him. He knew that. Given time in this beautiful place she loved, it would be the most natural thing in the world. He already had won her respect for his medical skill, he knew that. He also knew her eyes followed him wherever he went. At times he was convinced she loved him. Yet there was just enough doubt to worry him. So instead of pouring out the love he felt, he kept his kisses cool.

One night he dreamed an unknown fiancé popped up out of the nowhere — and woke sweating in spite of the chilly night! No, he would hold her to the engagement, and afterwards . . .

He couldn't go with the others to the Ice Festival. An employee had a heart attack and he felt he must stay and take care of him. Misty had volunteered to stay with him, but he told her, "There's nothing much to do. Go ahead and have fun." He pressed his lips lightly to hers and waved her off.

Yet when they came back, he couldn't deny the great leap of his heart. How could one small nurse have made such a big place for herself with him? At that moment he vowed to make her happy, to never cause her hurt or worry.

The days between the Ice Carnival and the wedding flew by. A man was brought in who had been hurt by one of the elk. Another case of getting too close, not remembering they were wild animals. Misty was glad for the work but sorry for the man.

In a few days he was all right. Still bruised from where he'd run and fallen, trying to get away from the elk, but all right. The only thing was, his vacation was spoiled.

He thanked Misty for her care with disillusioned eyes. "Next time I'll know enough to keep my distance." He asked her to sign his wrist cast and she did. "It will be Misty Rogers pretty soon now, I hear. Nice name."

It was a nice name. Misty hadn't thought of that. Now she stared after the departing patient. Misty Rogers. She would no longer be Misty McCall, in charge of her own life. She would be married, belong to another human being. Suddenly she panicked. What was she doing, marrying someone she didn't know loved her? Marriage to her had always been sacred, inviolate, with her own parents' example before her. Now she was deliberately walking into a mined field, marrying someone who perhaps only wanted a good housekeeper and nurse. A convenience.

It was the end. She could not do it. She tossed and turned all night and the next day awoke tireder than when she had gone to bed. Determinedly she got up, made a fire in her wood stove for the last time. The thought of it gave her a pang. Never again to make the wood fire, or curl up on her shabby couch. Tomorrow would have been her wedding day. It could never be. She would be compromising every ideal she had ever possessed if she went through with the wedding.

It didn't take long to pack. Hot tears scalded her cheeks as she selected just enough to fill an overnight case and a small suitcase, including uniforms. Maybe she could get Ginger to ship the rest of it after she got relocated.

Her fingers felt thick as she closed the door and locked it. Luckily Neil had gone to Livingston this morning. He wouldn't be expecting her on duty. She boarded the bus, scarcely seeing the brilliant winter world out the window. She saw Neil's face, a collage of memories that would haunt her forever. She saw the scenes of the past months, beautiful, dangerous, heartbreaking.

Her fingers crumpled the note she'd written and would mail in Livingston, the note she had labored over until she finally gave up and just wrote: "I can't marry a man I don't love. Please don't try and find me."

It was a lie, but it would save her pride. She had almost written, "I can't marry a man who doesn't love me," but she just couldn't do it.

The bus pulled into Gardiner, stopped. "We'll be ready to go on in a few minutes."

They seemed like eons of time to Misty, and yet as the driver boarded the bus, she frantically clutched her case and bag. "Wait, please! I've decided to get off."

What incredible impulse made her want to stop and see Ginger she couldn't explain. She could give Ginger the note. Ginger could tell Neil what she had done and why. It would be easier than just mailing the letter, less cowardly.

Misty never once thought Ginger might not be home. She was in such a state she didn't think of Ginger's job or anything. She just had to see her, as she had gone to her through training. Ginger was her "big sister." It might be childish, but Misty had no one else.

"What are you doing here?" Ginger came to the door in a heavy robe, her throat hoarse.

"I'm running away from home." The look on Misty's face took any triteness away from her statement.

"You're what?" Ginger pulled her inside.

Misty didn't see the furtive glance toward the

192

curtained-off kitchenette area, or the gently swaying drape that fell back in place.

"I'm running away. I'm going somewhere as far away as I can get, somewhere Neil Rogers can never find me."

Ginger actually turned white. Her freckles stood out on her beautiful skin. "But why, Misty, why? Tomorrow is your wedding day!"

"Was my wedding day. I'm not getting married." She swallowed a sob. "He doesn't love me, Ginger. He never did. You were wrong. All he wants is a housekeeper, a nurse to work with him, a convenience, and someday a mother for his children!"

She failed to note the little breeze in the room as the drape slid back, leaving an open passage into the kitchenette. She failed to see the someone who stood framed against it, motioning for Ginger not to betray the fact he was there.

"I've loved him ever since I can remember, once I got over being angry. When I thought he and Margie were more than friends, my whole world crashed. Then it got straightened out. Sometimes I think he does care for me a little. I had intended to go through with the wedding and take a chance on making him love me. But I can't do it, Ginger. Marriage is too important to me. If he didn't learn to love me, I would feel degraded, underhanded, trying to win his love that way."

Her voice was bitter, her eyes dull as she repeated, "All he wants is a convenience, not a wife."

"So that's what you think of me!"

Misty whirled. It couldn't be him. But it was! Dr. Neil Rogers was standing with arms crossed, watching her. She had never seen him colder in all the time she'd known him.

"What are you doing here?" she asked.

"I might ask you the same thing. I stopped in to ask Ginger something about our wedding on the way back from Livingston." Before either of the girls could reply, Dr. Rogers nodded to the bedroom door. "Ginger, if you will."

Ginger obeyed, probably more meekly than ever before in her life. It wasn't until she was inside with the heavy door closed that she leaned against it. "Ordered out of my own living room! Can you beat it? My own living room!"

But on the other side of the soundproof door, the two antagonists were not thinking of Ginger Snapp.

"So you really think all I want is a convenience."

"What else could I think?" Misty's shock was wearing off. Furiously she spurred her anger. She must never let him think she was begging. Even though he had obviously heard her own declaration of love, she didn't want his pity.

In one instant he had crossed the dividing space between them. His fingers bit into her arms, even through the heavy coat she wore. "Did you ever stop to think, Melissa McCall, that I might have ideals of my own? Did you ever realize that even in this day of easy love, come-

194

and-go affection, a man might be true to one woman? That he might love her with everything within him, want her not only for a wife but a companion, a helpmate, a joy through all the years until death do them part?"

His unconscious use of part of the wedding service did what nothing else could have done. Misty sagged.

"Look at me, Melissa McCall!" The man's voice rang out. "When you think I would marry you or any woman without love, you dishonor me!" His scorn lashed her. "I have loved you since before you even knew who I was. I went through hell on earth when you were hurt at Fishing Bridge. I died a thousand deaths when you were missing, when I knew Van Crandall had you!"

She had never seen him so angry. There was nothing cool about him now. His was righteous anger, directed at her. She could only hang loosely in his grip. Those steel fingers digging in her arms would leave bruises, but they were all that kept her from falling to the floor.

"You talk of love. You prattle to Ginger of going through a wedding and making me love you. Melissa McCall, you don't know the meaning of the first letter of the word love!" He dropped her.

Miraculously she kept to her feet. As he started through the door, he turned back. "If you can accept the kind of love I have for you, if you can stop being a ridiculous schoolgirl who clamors for pretty speeches, if you can become a woman, then tomorrow night at seven o'clock I'll be at the stone church." He stalked back to her. "This may help you decide."

His kisses were not cool this time. They rained on her face, burning out any doubt she might have had about him only wanting a convenience. Then as quickly as he had seized her, he let her go and walked out the door.

Misty never knew if it was minutes or hours before Ginger stuck her head out the bedroom door. "Is it safe to come out? I thought I heard a car door slam." She couldn't believe how Misty was just sitting there staring at the door. "Are you all right?"

"All right?" Misty found her voice. "Is someone who comes through a hurricane all right? I may never be all right again." She turned to Ginger with a wail. "Oh, Ginger, what have I done?"

What indeed? Ginger had a hard time making out what had happened from Misty's garbled explanation. "Hadn't trusted him . . . dishonored him . . . he had ideals . . . I didn't know what love was . . . no pretty speeches from him . . . be at church if I can grow up . . ."

At that point Ginger shook her hard. "You mean to say after all your lack of trust, he will still marry you? Misty, you little idiot, he must love you more than you deserve. After standing there hearing your indictment of him —" She shook her head.

"How could I think anything else?" Once more Misty was regaining her natural spirit. Her eyes flashed. "Why didn't he tell me how he felt? Margie even told me he carries around a picture of himself and some girl! What could I think?"

"I think you'd better get ready to catch the next bus back to Mammoth. I'm sure you must have things to do to get ready for your wedding."

Misty stared, then stood up. "I do. One very important thing." As she stepped out the door she repeated, "One very important thing."

Oh, no, what was she up to now? But Ginger had gone as far as she could. Whatever Misty planned, it would have to be on her own. Ginger was tired and had to get over a cold she'd caught. Boy, she'd never before appreciated how good she had it with Frank. If they'd had to go through all this — She grimaced and headed for the bathroom. A good soak in a hot tub should take some of the cold out of her.

There was a light knock on the door that evening. Neil rose to cross the firelit room. He had been sitting watching the blaze, feeling uncertain. Would Misty come back? So she should have had more faith in him. He shouldn't have yelled at her like that. There was a dull ache inside. He had looked forward to spending this last evening before their wedding, alone and thoughtful, thinking of all the years they would share together. Instead, there was this fear there wouldn't be any wedding.

"May I come in?"

He stared disbelievingly at the small girl on his doorstep, then silently swung the door wide. She removed her snowflake-covered cap, her heavy mittens, her sturdy boots, and then deliberately walked to the fireplace.

"I've come —" She looked at him, unable to continue. If only he would help her.

His face was impassive, shuttered against her imploring gaze. "You've come to tell me you don't want to marry me."

"No!"

He kept his arms crossed, judge and jury all in one. If he weakened now, everything would be lost. He would tell her he had no intention of ever letting her go, even if he had to pull a Van Crandall stunt and carry her off!

"I'll marry you, on one condition," she said.

"And just what is this condition of yours?"

She just couldn't take it anymore. "You wooden Indian! How can you stand there like that? You said you cared about me, then help me out!"

It didn't seem to faze him at all. "The condition?"

She blindly thrust out the words that had rankled so long. "Margie said you carry a picture of yourself and — and some girl. I want to see that picture."

So that was it. Relief flooded him. Deep inside the ice chunk that had been his heart — since he'd discovered her at Ginger's — began to melt. He froze up again. "Certainly not. You will see the picture *after* you are married to me." He paused and eyed her. "By the way, we will exchange confidences. You can tell me all about the little message Margie was to carry but didn't."

The whiteness of her face was marred by a sharp thrust of color. "But why?" She came closer, looking into his face. "Why must you hold this over my head?"

"I want you to trust me, Misty." There was pain in his voice.

She thought of the times her faith had wavered, suddenly realizing the depths of this man she loved. It decided her.

"All right, Neil. I will." Her eyes were clear, without deceit. It almost unnerved him. After all they had gone through, to have her stand there looking at him like that!

He stooped, caught her close. This time the kiss was tender. "I'll walk you home."

The stone chapel was alive with red roses and candlelight. The age-old words of the marriage service rang from the walls that had seen countless other couples exchange vows there. Misty looked beautiful. Gone was all sign of havoc, mistrust. She had promised to have faith in Neil; now she entrusted her life and happiness into his keeping.

When they came out of the church, it was starting to snow.

"We'll have to get back," Ginger said, hugging them both.

The others followed suit. Misty's heart pounded. She was married. Mrs. Doctor Neil Rogers. Misty Rogers. It had a nice ring.

"I love you, Misty." Her new husband had carried her over the threshold and into the living room with its already laid fire. He put her down, touched a match to the kindling, and flames shot high. "Now it's time to settle the last things between us. Will you go first? Just what did you tell Margie that day?"

She hadn't known he could be so gentle. "I had to send word. I couldn't die out there somewhere letting you think I had been engaged to anyone else. You are the only man I've ever loved, Neil."

She was too engrossed with her story to note the dark color staining his face. "The only way I knew to do it was to send a message you could understand. I told Marge, 'Tell Dr. Rogers I won't be able to accept his proposition on account of a sudden engagement.' I knew you'd know it was the engagement with Van Crandall, being carried off."

For a moment they were silent, reliving that awful night and the day following. Then Misty stirred within the circle of his arms. "Now it's your turn."

Neil didn't answer for a moment. He was too filled with happiness. Even in her extremity Misty had tried to send him a message of love. But a fleeting memory of how he had suffered when he heard her lack of faith in him, her feeling he only wanted a housekeeper, made him decide. There was one more thing he would do.

Slowly he reached in his pocket, brought out his wallet. He didn't open it, but balanced it on his hand, as if weighing just what to say. "Misty, I'm afraid this is going to come as a shock to you. After all we've been through, I hate to tell you. Yet it's only fair for you to know." He nearly choked at the hypocrisy in his own voice. She would detect it, surely!

She didn't. She was looking at him with wide eyes, wondering what was coming.

"Margie was right. I do carry a picture of a girl. A very special girl. She was my first love."

Misty's mind whirled. It wasn't reasonable to expect she had been Neil's first love, as he had been hers. Yet for one moment she hated the girl whose picture he carried. How could she look at it and not betray herself? Why had she insisted he show it to her?

The look in her eyes was not unnoticed by Neil. He had his revenge. Never again would he put her to the test, but now it swept away forever the last bit of hurt she had inflicted. "Open it, Mrs. Rogers."

With fingers trembling slightly, Misty opened the wallet. She gasped. His first love. He stood beside her, tall and strong. But it was not on the man's image Misty's eyes rested. It was on his companion. Hate her? Impossible. She should have listened more closely when Margie said she had not taken a good look at the picture. They stood against the clinic right here in Mammoth. Evidently the picture had been taken in the summer. There were flowers and trees for a background. Neil's first love, and thank God, his last. For the girl in the picture he had carried for all those months was Misty McCall.

The employees of G.K. Hall hope you have enjoyed this Large Print book. All our Large Print titles are designed for easy reading, and all our books are made to last. Other G.K. Hall books are available at your library, through selected bookstores, or directly from us.

For information about titles, please call:

(800) 257-5157

To share your comments, please write:

Publisher
G.K. Hall & Co.
P.O. Box 159
Thorndike, ME 04986